STORIES

for

INFANTS

AT HOME AND SCHOOL

compiled by

D. M. PRESCOTT

BLANDFORD PRESS

POOLE   DORSET

First published 1967
© 1967 Blandford Press Ltd.,
Link House, West Street, Poole, Dorset, BH15 1LL
Revised edition 1974
Reprinted 1978

ISBN 0 7137 0687 2

Printed in Great Britain by
Fletcher & Son Ltd, Norwich

CONTENTS

3

4   *Contents*

Section 4   Nature

Section 5   Myths and Legends

Section 6   Times and Seasons

Spring (Easter)

Summer (Holidays)

Autumn (Harvest)

Winter (Christmas)

Section 7 Simple Stories from History

THE BLANDFORD SERIES
OF ASSEMBLY BOOKS

Edited by D. M. Prescott

The Senior Teacher's Assembly Book
The Senior Teacher's Prayer Book
Readings for the Senior Assembly
More Readings for the Senior Assembly

The Junior Teacher's Assembly Book
The Junior Teacher's Prayer Book
Stories for the Junior Assembly
More Stories for the Junior Assembly
Further Stories for the Junior Assembly
Poems for the School Assembly

The Infant Teacher's Assembly Book
The Infant Teacher's Prayer Book
Stories for Infants at Home and at School

ACKNOWLEDGEMENTS

The editor wishes to thank contributors who have written stories especially for this book, and the publishers who have given permission to use existing material. Acknowledgement is given at the foot of each story.

Every effort has been made to trace copyright ownership, and it is regretted if any acknowledgements have been omitted.

PREFACE

The stories in this book are suitable either to read or to tell. Some are modern, some old-fashioned; but all contain the necessary material which teachers can use as desired. And all have character-building value.

There are seven sections. The first contains stories of fact, many of them based on actual happenings. When this is so, the story is marked to that effect. The second section is fantasy, both old and new. Many people today are coming to realise, contrary to what has been taught in recent years, that fantasy is an essential ingredient in a child's development. The third section contains stories based on nursery rhymes, and the fourth stories from nature. The fifth is a collection of myths and legends, many of them retold in simple language, rather than in the stilted style in which they so often seem to be written. 'Times and Seasons', the sixth section, has stories appropriate to the four seasons of the year, together with the special occasions associated with them—Easter, Holidays, Harvest and Christmas. The final section is a small group of very simple stories from history, which has been asked for specially for the older infants.

In each section the stories have been graded, to start simply and build up to more mature treatment. Teachers using them will know what degree of complexity will be required by the particular children in question. There are one or two somewhat more sophisticated stories, such as 'The test' on page 93, or 'A hole in your stocking' on page 89; it has been found that certain groups of children are quite capable of appreciating these, and so they have been included, especially in view of the more flexible age of transfer envisaged in the Plowden report.

There are two stories by children on pages 130 and 133. Anne Frank, who died so tragically at the age of 16 and whose *Diary* will be known by many, wrote a number of

9

stories for children. One of these is included in this book, on page 105.

There is an alphabetical index and a subject index. Teachers will find that a number of the stories are suitable for dramatic treatment.

It is hoped that this book will be a useful source of supply on which to draw on those many occasions when the teacher says, 'Now I'll tell you a story.' They will also be a help to parents, especially at bedtime!

D.M.P.

I

STORIES OF FACT

John and Jane were playing outside their house one day when their mother called, 'John and Jane, come here a minute.'

So they ran in, and their mother said, 'I want you to go shopping for me. I want you to buy a small bag of flour and a small bottle of salad cream. Here is the money; and here is extra money to buy yourselves some sweets.'

So off they went. They went first to the grocer's and bought the flour and the salad cream. Then they went to the sweet shop to buy the sweets. They looked and looked to see what sweets they would like, and at last they chose some little chocolate drops, because they thought there would be a nice lot of them. Then off they went home. John carried the bag of flour, and Jane carried the bottle of salad cream; they kept passing the bag of sweets from one to the other, and each taking one in turn.

Presently John said, 'Jane, you've had more than your share.'

'No, I haven't,' said Jane.

'Yes, you have.'

'No, I haven't.'

'Yes, you *have*!' And John made a grab at the bag. Jane snatched it away, and a fight began. John gave Jane a punch which made her drop the bottle of salad cream. It fell on the ground and smashed, and the salad cream was spattered all over her shoes and socks. They went on tussling, and presently John dropped the bag of flour too. It burst, and out came a cloud of flour which settled all over the children.

When they saw what had happened they stopped fighting, and looked at each other. They *were* in a mess! So slowly and sadly they went home, and told their mother what had happened. They had to be washed and put into clean clothes; and their mother said, 'I thought I had two sensible children; but I've only got two babies after all.'

'Oh, Mummy, do let us go again,' they cried. So their mother forgave them, and did let them go again; and this time they managed to bring the flour and the salad cream safely home. And their mother can really trust them to do the shopping now.

ANNIE AND NANNIE AND SALLY AND SUE

This is the story of four little girls. Their names were Annie and Nannie and Sally and Sue.

One day they were talking about which of them was the best.

'I am the biggest,' said Annie. 'Look how high I can jump! And look how hard I can push the swing!'

'I am the cleverest,' said Nannie. 'Look what good drawings I did at school. Teacher said they were the best.'

'I am the prettiest,' said Sally. 'Look at the blue bows in my hair and my pretty dress.'

But little Sue said nothing at all, because she had nothing to say.

Then one day the little girls' grandpa came to see them. He sat in a chair, and all the little girls stood round him.

'I am the biggest,' said Annie; and she told about the high jump and the hard push.

'I am the cleverest,' said Nannie; and she told about the drawings at school.

'I am the prettiest,' said Sally; and she showed Grandpa her blue bows and her pretty dress.

But little Sue said nothing at all, because she had nothing to say. She only climbed on Grandpa's knee, because that was where she liked to be.

Then they all had tea; and while they were eating Annie

talked about high jumps and big pushes; and Nannie talked about reading and writing and drawing at school; and Sally talked about all the pretty dresses she was going to have one day. But little Sue said nothing at all, because she had nothing to say. She only passed Grandpa the bread and butter, and the cake, and the sugar for his tea, and picked up his stick when it fell down, because that was what she liked to do.

And after tea, when Grandpa was ready to go home, he said to the four little girls, 'You are the biggest, Annie; and you are the cleverest, Nannie; and you are the prettiest, Sally; but my little Sue is the kindest, and that is the best of all.'

KEVIN AND BABY SISTER

This is a story about a little boy called Kevin and his baby sister. Baby Sister was still very small; she couldn't walk yet.

One day Kevin went out to play in the garden. He played for a long while, until he had a dinner-time sort of feeling inside him.

'I'll go in,' he thought, 'and see if dinner is ready.'

But when he got indoors, he heard a loud noise. 'Oh dear,' he thought, 'that's Baby Sister crying.' He went into the room where the noise was, and there was Baby Sister crying and crying, and there was Mummy holding her and trying and trying to hush her.

'What's the matter with Baby Sister, Mummy?' asked Kevin.

'I don't know,' said Mummy. 'She hasn't got a pin sticking into her, because I looked; and she isn't tired, because she's just had a lovely sleep.'

'Perhaps she's hungry,' said Kevin.

'Well, if she is,' said Mummy, 'I don't see how I'm going to get her any dinner while she's screaming like this. Kevin, you see what you can do with her.'

'All right,' said Kevin; and he went up to Baby Sister and said, 'Boo!'

Baby Sister was so surprised that she stopped crying and stared at Kevin.

So Kevin said 'Boo!' again, and then Baby Sister smiled.

'Boo!' said Kevin again, and this time Baby Sister laughed. Then Kevin laughed, and then Baby Sister laughed, and then they both laughed. They laughed and laughed and *laughed!*

'Kevin,' said his mummy, 'if I put you and Baby Sister in the big armchair together, do you think you could keep her happy while I finish getting the dinner?'

'Oh yes, Mummy,' said Kevin. So he and Baby Sister sat in the big chair together, and Kevin talked to her and sang to her and told her stories. Baby Sister didn't understand it all, but she liked it very much, and she sat quite good and quiet till Mummy came in to say dinner was ready.

'There's my big boy,' said Mummy. 'Whatever should I do without you, Kevin?' She picked up Baby Sister, and said to her, 'Aren't you a lucky girl to have a kind big brother to look after you so nicely?'

And Kevin felt very pleased, and very big and important.

And then they all had their dinner.

THE LITTLE RED CANDLE

Bobby had a little sister called Betty, and she was just going to be four years old. The day before Betty's birthday, Bobby went into the kitchen and found his mother cooking.

'What are you making, Mummy?' he asked.

'I am making a birthday cake for Betty,' she said. 'When it is baked, I shall put lovely white icing on it.'

On the table near by was a small paper bag. Bobby peeped inside and saw some little red candles. They looked so bright and gay that he longed to have one for his own. So he took one out of the bag. 'I shall keep this,' he thought; and he went upstairs and put it away in the little box where he kept his treasures.

The next day he went into the kitchen again. There on the

table was a lovely cake, and he saw that his mother had put the white icing all over it, and now she was writing Betty's name on it very carefully in red sugar letters. Bobby could read them—'B-E-T-T-Y'.

Then his mother said, 'Now I must put the candles on.' She picked up the paper bag and took out the little red candles. 'Why,' she cried, 'there are only three. There ought to be four, because Betty is going to be four years old. Where can the other one be? I know I had exactly four left.' She hunted all over the table, and on the floor under it, but of course she couldn't find the fourth little red candle. (Do you remember where it was?) 'Oh dear,' she said, 'what a pity! The birthday cake will be quite spoiled, and I have no time to go out and buy another candle.'

Now by this time Bobby was feeling very unhappy inside. He did so want to keep the little red candle. He thought about it, and he thought about it, all the time he was eating his dinner. He *did* want the candle—but he also wanted Betty to have a nice birthday party and a cake with four candles on it. So at last he went upstairs and took the little red candle out of his treasure box and brought it downstairs to the kitchen.

'Here it is, Mummy,' he said. 'I took it, and I'm sorry. Now you can put it on the cake.'

So Bobby's mother took the little red candle and put it on the white icing with the other three. And it did look nice there. And when Betty saw her cake at her birthday party, how pleased she was! She counted the red candles—one, two, three, four—all alight and shining. And then she blew them all out with one great blow—*pouf!*

HELPFUL BRIAN

Based on a true story

This is the story of a little boy called Brian, who was only four years old. He lived with his father and mother in the country, and near his house there was a farm. The farmer was called Mr. Jones, and he had a great many sheep.

Brian loved to go to the field where the sheep were and watch them. He specially liked looking at the little lambs, and seeing them jumping and frisking about and playing together, and then running back to their mothers.

One day, when Brian's father came in to his tea, he said, 'Farmer Jones is very worried about his sheep. There is a big dog that comes into their field and chases them and frightens them, and nobody can catch him. Mr. Jones has asked the police to help him, and they want anyone who sees this dog chasing the sheep to tell them.'

Brian thought a lot about that. He was very sorry for the poor sheep who were so frightened by the big dog, and especially for the little lambs. He hoped that someone would soon catch the bad dog and stop him doing it. 'If I see that dog,' he said to himself, 'I shall tell our policeman.' The policeman was a very kind man. He lived near Brian's house, and he and Brian were very good friends.

Then one day, when Brian was watching the sheep over a hedge, he did see the bad dog. There it was, running to and fro and barking and jumping up and down, and the sheep were baa-ing and running all over the field, and the little lambs were crying after their mothers.

'What shall I do?' thought Brian. He looked down the road, and what do you think he saw? His own policeman friend coming along on his bicycle. Wasn't that lucky? Brian waved to him and pointed over the hedge, and made signs to him to be very quiet. The policeman jumped off his bicycle and leaned it against the hedge and came to look.

'Oho!' he said. 'So that's the bad dog.' He jumped over the hedge and tried to catch it, but of course it ran away. 'Never mind,' he said when he came back to Brian, 'I know who he is. He is the big black-and-white dog who belongs to Mr. Smith down the road. I will go and tell him that he must chain his dog up so that it can't get at the sheep any more, and if he takes it out it must go on a lead. Well done, Brian!' And he went back with Brian to Brian's home and told his mother how pleased he was that Brian had been so helpful, even though he was such a little boy.

COLIN'S CLEVER IDEA

Based on a true story

One day Colin's mummy said to him, 'I have to go out to the shop across the road to get some milk.'

'Can I come too?' asked Colin.

'No,' said his mummy. 'You have had a nasty cold; it is better now, but I don't want you to go out in the cold till it is quite well. But you can watch me from the window.'

So she went out and shut the front door. And Colin climbed up on the window-seat and watched. He saw his mummy go across the road and into the shop, and after a little while she came out with a bottle of milk, and he saw her come back again across the road to the front door.

Colin got down off the window-seat and waited for the door to open. But it didn't open; and presently Colin heard a funny rattling noise. He went out into the hall, and saw that the flap of the letter-box was jumping up and down all by itself.

Then he heard someone calling, 'Colin! Colin!' At first he didn't know where the voice was coming from; but then he knew that it was his mummy's voice, and that she was talking to him through the letter-box.

'Colin,' she was saying. 'Can you hear me?'

'Yes, Mummy,' said Colin. 'I can hear you.'

Then his mummy said, 'I have left the front-door key behind in the house, and I can't get in. Will you look and see if you can find the key and give it to me through the letter-box?'

So Colin looked everywhere—in the sitting-room, and

in the kitchen, and in the bedroom, and even in the bath-room; but he couldn't find that key *anywhere*.

'I can't find it, Mummy,' he called through the letter-box.

'Oh dear,' said his mummy. 'Whatever shall we do? Perhaps I can borrow a ladder from Mrs. Brown next door. Then I can climb in through the upstairs window.'

Then she went away, and Colin was left all alone; and he felt very lonely. And then he had a clever idea. He went into the kitchen, where the back door was. He pulled a chair up to the back door, and climbed up on it, and there was the back door key sticking in the keyhole. Colin caught hold of it, and tried to turn it. It was rather stiff, but he went on trying, and slowly, slowly it turned.

Then he got down off the chair, and pulled it away from the back door. And then he heard his mummy rattling the letter-box again. He ran into the hall, and heard her calling, 'I can't find Mrs. Brown—she must be out. So I'll go and find a policeman to help us.'

'No, Mummy,' Colin called back. 'Go round to the back door. I've opened it.'

'What did you say, Colin?' asked his mummy. She couldn't believe what he said. But she went round to the back door, and turned the door handle, and—the door opened and in she came! 'What a clever idea, Colin! Why didn't I think of doing that?' she said.

THE LITTLE WHISPER

Based on a true story

Jane and Susan lived in the country. One day it was Jane's birthday, and their granny came to see them.

'Jane,' said Granny, 'I am going to buy you a little donkey as a birthday present.'

'Oh, Granny—how lovely!' cried Jane.

'That is very kind of you, Granny,' said Jane and Susan's mother.

Nobody saw Susan sitting in the corner. Her mouth was going down, down, down at the corners, until suddenly, 'Boo! Hoo! I want a donkey too!' sobbed Susan. She cried and she cried and she cried, till at last her mother had to take her into another room. She took Susan on her knee and said, 'Susan, do you know why you are crying?'

'Because Jane has a donkey and I haven't got one,' sobbed Susan.

'No,' said her mother, 'it is because of the little whisper.'

'The little whisper?' said Susan. She was so surprised that she stopped crying.

'Yes,' said her mother. 'Didn't you hear it? It whispered in your ear, "It's not fair! Jane has a donkey and you haven't." And that's what made you cry.'

'Did it really whisper? Did you hear it, Mummy?' asked Susan.

'No,' said her mother. 'I didn't hear it just then. But I have heard it at other times.'

'Have you really?' said Susan. 'What did it say?'

'Do you remember,' said her mother, 'when Auntie Ethel came to tea in that lovely new fur coat? When I saw it, the little whisper said to me, "It isn't fair: Why should she have a coat like that and not you?" '

'And what did you do, Mummy?' asked Jane. 'Did you cry, like me?'

'No, I didn't cry,' said her mother. 'I just said, "I hear you, little whisper. But I'm not going to listen to you—you can just pop off!" '

'And did it go?' asked Susan.

'Yes,' said her mother. 'That little jealous whisper always goes away if you say you aren't going to listen.'

'Horrid little whisper!' said Susan. 'I'm not going to listen to it—ever!'

The next day Jane's donkey came. Her name was Biddy,

and she was put in the paddock. Jane and Susan went to see her, and they had rides on her in turn. Susan loved that—it was almost as nice as having a donkey of your very own.

The next morning the little girls' mother came into their room and said, 'Jane, Susan, get up and dress quickly, and come and see what is in the paddock with Biddy.' So up they jumped, and soon they were running over the grass to where Biddy was. And there beside Biddy was something else. It was—it was——

'Why, it's a baby donkey,' cried Susan.

'Yes,' said their mother. 'We had no idea that Biddy was going to have a little foal. But now that she has it, it shall be your donkey, Susan; and when it is big enough, you and Jane can both ride your donkeys together.'

'Hurrah! Hurrah!' cried Susan and Jane.

TINA'S TEDDY

Tina had a teddy, and she loved him very much. Teddy was very old, and he had been hugged and squeezed so much that he was quite thin, and his arms and legs were all floppy; but Tina loved him just the same.

One morning Tina's mummy said, 'Shall we go out shopping?'

'Oh yes,' said Tina. 'Teddy loves shopping.'

So off they went. Mummy had a big basket on wheels, and Tina had a little basket. And inside the little basket sat Teddy, looking out at the great big world all round him.

First they went to the butcher's to buy some sausages. Then they went to the grocer's to buy tea and sugar and lots of other things. Then they went to the baker's to buy some bread and some cakes for tea. And then they went to the draper's to buy a new blue hair band for Tina. And Mummy put all these things in the big basket on wheels—all except Tina's new hair band, because she wanted to carry that herself.

'We've just got time,' said Mummy, 'to pop into the library and get a book for Tony,' Tony was Tina's brother, and he was at school. So they went in, and while Mummy was looking for a book about engines for Tony, Tina found a lovely book all about kittens. But she had only just started looking at the pictures when Mummy said, 'Come on, Tina —quick! We've only just got time to catch our bus.' They had to run for it, and jumped in just as the bus was starting. And it was then that Tina said, 'Oh, Mummy—I haven't got Teddy.'

'Oh, darling, he must have fallen out of the basket somewhere,' said Mummy.

'We must go back and look for him,' said Tina; and she began to sob.

'All right, said Mummy. 'As soon as we've had our dinner, we'll go back to all the shops we went to, and see if he is there. You must help me to remember where we went.'

And that's what they did. They went to the butcher's where they had bought the sausages; and they went to the grocer's where they had bought the tea and sugar; and they went to the baker's where they had bought the bread and cakes; and they went to the draper's where they had bought Tina's new blue hair band. But Teddy wasn't in any of those shops.

'Oh, Mummy, Mummy, Teddy's lost!' said Tina, and she began to cry loudly, right there in the street.

'Let's think hard,' said Mummy. 'Is there any other place we went to?' So Tina stopped crying and thought hard. And then she said, 'Oh yes, the place where I saw the book about the kittens.'

'Oh, of course—the library,' said her mummy. 'How stupid of me to forget.' So they hurried to the library—and there on the desk sat Teddy, waiting for Tina. She snatched him up and hugged him.

'I'm so glad you came back for him,' said the lady behind

the desk. 'We found him, but we didn't know your name, so we just had to wait and hope you would come.'

And Tina was telling Teddy how very, very, *very* glad she was to see him again.

ROSIE'S FLAG

Everyone was very excited in Rosie's house. The Queen was coming to their town, and they were all going out to wave to her as she went by—Mummy and Daddy and Auntie Eileen and Grandma and Bobby and Billy—and Rosie too, of course.

The day before the Queen was coming, Rosie's daddy came in with some wooden sticks, and on the top of each stick was a piece of stuff with a pattern of lines and crosses on it in red, white and blue.

'What are those, Daddy?' asked Rosie.

'They are Union Jacks,' he said. 'The Union Jack is the special flag for British people, like all of us in this house. The boys and girls will be waving them tomorrow when the Queen goes by. So I have bought one for Bobby and one for Billy and a little one for you, Rosie.'

Rosie was very, very pleased with her flag. She practised waving it and cheering, and when she was in bed, there was the flag tucked in beside her and lying on her pillow.

In the morning they all started out very early to see the Queen. Rosie held her flag tightly as they walked along. Then they had to go on a bus. Rosie put her flag down on an empty seat beside her. Bobby and Billy were very excited, and they kept jumping about on the seats, and then—oh dear! Billy sat right down on Rosie's flag! There was a snapping sound, and there was the stick broken in two. Poor Rosie began to cry. 'Now I haven't got anything to wave for the Queen,' she sobbed.

Rosie's mother was very cross with Billy. 'You shouldn't be so careless,' she said. 'Well, Rosie shouldn't have left it on the seat,' said Billy. 'It was her fault.' 'Never mind, Rosie,' said Bobby, who was a kind brother. 'You can have a turn with my flag and wave that if you like.' But Rosie went on crying. 'I want my own flag,' she said, and she sobbed and sobbed.

At last they got to the place where they were to wait to see the Queen. There were lots and lots of other people there, but they let Bobby and Billy and Rosie go right through to the front so that they could see. And there they stood waiting for the Queen to come. It seemed a long time to wait; but there were soldiers to look at, and sandwiches to eat, and a man on a beautiful black horse kept riding up and down. Rosie still wished she had her flag, but there was so much to see that she forgot about it and began to enjoy herself. Anyway, Bobby had said she could have a turn waving his flag.

Then suddenly, as she was looking about her, she saw something. A man was coming along, and he was carrying lots and lots of Union Jacks.

'Oh, look, look, Daddy!' cried Rosie. The man came up, and Daddy put his hand in his pocket. He took out some money and gave it to the man. And the man gave Rosie a flag just like the one that was broken.

And then the Queen came driving slowly by, in a big car that was open so that everyone could see her. She had a pretty hat on all covered with flowers, and she was smiling and waving her hand. All the people were cheering and waving, and Rosie waved and waved her Union Jack, and she shouted 'Hooray!' with all her might. And, do you know, the Queen heard her. She gave Rosie a special wave and smile all to herself. Wasn't Rosie lucky?

JEREMY AND THE WALKER

Based on a true story

Jeremy didn't like walks. Whenever his mother said, 'We're going for a walk now, Jeremy,' he always said, 'Need we?'

in a whiny sort of voice. But they always went. Jeremy didn't
enjoy the walks, and his mother didn't enjoy them either—
Jeremy was so grumpy all the way.

One day Jeremy's mother took him to see the doctor.
The doctor, who was a nice kind man, poked Jeremy a little
bit, and said, 'Young man, you're getting too fat. Too many
sweets, I expect. What you need is more exercise.'

'What's exercise?' asked Jeremy.

'Walks,' said the doctor.

'Oh,' said Jeremy. 'Bother.'

So he went for still more walks, and he didn't like that at
all. Then one day his Uncle Bob came to visit them. Jeremy
loved Uncle Bob, and he always told him things. So now he
told Uncle Bob about all the horrid walks.

'Bad luck,' said Uncle Bob. 'Never mind, Jeremy—I'll tell
you what I'll do. Next time I come I'll bring you a walker.'

'A walker?' said Jeremy. 'What's that?'

'Something to help you to walk,' said Uncle Bob.

'Do you mean a sort of a machine?' asked Jeremy.

'You'll see when I bring it,' said Uncle Bob.

'Will it hurt?' asked Jeremy.

'No,' said Uncle Bob.

'Shall I like it?'

'Yes, you will.'

'When will you bring it?'

'Next Saturday.'

All the days before Saturday, Jeremy was thinking about
the walker and wondering what it would be like. Like a
car, or a bicycle, or a basket on wheels like the one Mummy
took out shopping, or the little trolley Grandma used for her
luggage? But none of those would help him to walk. They
would only do the walking for him.

At last it was Saturday, and Uncle Bob's car drove up to
the door. Jeremy ran out to meet him.

'Have you brought it, Uncle Bob?' he called out.

'Yes, here it is,' said his uncle, bringing out a little basket.

'It's very small,' said Jeremy. 'What's it like?'

'Come indoors, and I'll show you,' said Uncle Bob. So they went in, and Uncle Bob put the basket on the table and opened it, and inside was a little puppy! It looked up at them and barked.

'Is *that* a walker?' said Jeremy.

'Yes,' said Uncle Bob. 'He has to have a walk every day, and you'll have to take him, and that will give you a walk too. So he'll be your walker.'

'I shan't mind *that* kind of walk,' said Jeremy. 'Can I take him out now?'

'Yes,' said Uncle Bob. 'But we must put him on a lead first.' So they put the little dog on a lead, and then he and Jeremy went for a walk—or rather, a run—the little dog pulled so hard that Jeremy had to run to keep up. When they got back he was panting for breath.

'I'm going to call him Toots,' he said. And every day after that he and Toots went for a long walk together. And the next time Jeremy's mother took him to the doctor, the doctor said, 'You're much thinner now, young man. How have you done it?'

'It was the walker,' said Jeremy.

'The walker—what's that?' asked the doctor. So then Jeremy told him all about Toots.

'I wish more of my patients had walkers like that,' said the doctor. 'Then they would look as fit and well as you do.'

WHAT JENNIFER FOUND

Jennifer was going for a walk with her grandfather, in her new blue-and-white dress with the two blue pockets in front. Jennifer loved going for walks with Grandpa. They always went on Saturday, and they always did the same things. First they went to the pond. Jennifer had a bag of crusts, and they fed the ducks. Sometimes there were boys sailing boats on the pond, and Jennifer loved to watch them.

After that she and Grandpa sat on a special seat while he told her a story; and after *that* Jennifer played by herself while Grandpa had a little nap.

This day they did all their usual things. They went to the pond, and the ducks gobbled up the crusts with loud quackings. There were two boys sailing boats, and one boat got stuck in the middle of the pond. But Grandpa lent the boy his stick, and he managed to get it back. Then they sat on their special seat, and Grandpa told Jennifer a story about two little mice. Then Jennifer ran off to play with her red ball while Grandpa had his nap. She tried to see how far she could throw the ball, and she threw it such a long way that it bounced into some deep grass and she couldn't see it. She poked and peered in the grass, and under some bushes near by; but she couldn't find it. But she found something else— something bright and shining hidden in the grass. She pulled it out, and it was round and twisty and had little bits of something shiny all over it. They flashed so much in the sun that Jennifer was quite dazzled.

'What a pretty thing!' she thought. 'I shall take it home and keep it with my other precious things in the box with roses on the lid.' So she put it in one of her blue pockets and ran back to Grandpa. 'Hullo, Jennifer,' he said. 'Time to start for home.'

As they walked along the street, Grandpa said, 'I think I'll stop at the police station and look at the notice-board to see if there are any interesting notices on it.' So they stopped and looked. There were lots of notices. Grandpa read out one about someone who had lost a little dog. And then he said, 'Oh, dear, some poor lady has lost her diamond brooch. She offers a reward to anyone who finds it.'

'What is a diamond brooch?' asked Jennifer.

'It is a piece of jewellery to pin on your dress,' said Grandpa. 'It is made of silver or gold, and the diamonds are tiny stones which shine very brightly.'

Jennifer thought of what was in her pocket. She had

wanted so much to keep it! But she knew she must show it to Grandpa.

'Is it like this?' she asked, and held out the bright thing.

'Why, bless me, child,' said her grandfather, 'that looks like the very thing! We'll go to the lady's house—it isn't very far away—and ask if it is.'

So they went to a big house in a lovely garden, and Grandpa rang the doorbell. A lady came to the door, and when she saw the brooch she cried, 'Oh, my brooch! Wherever did you find it?'

'My little granddaughter found it,' said Grandpa, 'in some long grass.' So then Jennifer told where she had seen it, and the lady said, 'I must have dropped it when I was looking at a little bird in the bushes. But come in, come in.' So in they went, and the lady gave Jennifer some lemonade, and she gave Grandpa a piece of paper which he put away very carefully in his pocket.

'What is that paper, Grandpa?' asked Jennifer as they started home.

'It is the reward for finding the brooch,' said her grandfather. 'It is a cheque for a lot of money. It doesn't always happen that if you find something you get a reward; but you were lucky this time. Some of the money we will put in the savings bank for you till you are older, and some of it you shall spend on anything you like.'

On the next Saturday, Jennifer and her grandfather did not go to the park. Instead they went to the toy shop to choose the reward. And what do you think Jennifer bought? A lovely dolly's pram to wheel her dolls and her teddies about in. She had wanted one for a long time, and now she had one for her very own.

WHAT SHALL WE CALL THE BABY?

Tony had a new baby sister, and he thought she was the sweetest and the funniest little person he had ever seen. She had black hair which stood up on her head in a little tuft, and when she was awake—which wasn't very often—she had blue, blue eyes which kept looking and looking at him as if she were trying to find out all about this big brother of hers. But there was one very funny thing about her—she had no name. Tony's daddy and mummy just could not decide what to call her.

They were talking about it one day, when Tony was sitting on the floor playing with his toy engine.

'We really must decide on Baby's name,' said his mother.

'I thought we had decided,' said his father. 'She's to be called Jane, after my mother, her granny.'

'But that's such an old-fashioned, short little name,' said his mother. 'I should like her to be called Belinda.'

'I think that's a very fanciful sort of name,' said Tony's father. 'Anyway, I more or less promised Granny we would call her Jane. It would make Granny so happy to know that our baby had the same name as herself.'

'Well, it would make me happy if the baby was called Belinda,' said his mother.

Tony was listening to all this. He liked both the names—they both seemed just right for his sweet little baby sister. And then he had an idea.

'Mummy—Daddy——' he said. 'Shall I tell you what I think?'

'Why, of course, Tony,' said his mother.

'I think,' said Tony, 'that she should have *both* names. Then Granny would be pleased, and Mummy would be pleased too, and everybody would be happy.'

'Why, Tony, that's a splendid idea!' cried his mother. 'Belinda Jane! Yes, that's a very nice name.'

'Good for you, Tony, old boy,' said his father. 'Why ever didn't we think of asking you before? Belinda Jane it shall be.'

And Tony felt very proud and pleased that he had been able to help in giving his baby sister her name.

TOM AND TOBY

A true story

Many years ago, on an Australian farm, there lived two dogs called Tom and Toby. They were sheep-dogs, and Tom was black, while Toby was black and tan, with white forepaws and chest.

In the house where they lived there was a baby boy, and Tom and Toby were his favourite playmates. They looked after him, too, from the time he was a baby; and when he started to learn to walk, he would grab hold of Tom's hair on one side, and Toby's hair on the other, and pull himself up and then stagger along between them. The dogs loved him, and whenever they were not busy at their work with the sheep, they would be playing with the little boy. His mother always knew that he was perfectly safe when he was with them.

As he grew a little older, and could walk and run, he and the dogs would go out for walks together, and have marvellous games, playing with a ball or pretending to dig up rabbits. But always the dogs brought him safely home for his evening meal.

But one evening, when the men came in from their work, there was no little boy to be seen, and no Tom or Toby either. Where could they be? Everyone went out to search, but none of the three was to be found. All that night they hunted, and all the next day, and the next night too; but neither boy nor dogs could be found. The poor mother cried till she could cry no more.

Then, just as the second day began to dawn, the mother heard a scratching and crying at the door. There was Tom, jumping and whining and licking her hands, and then running off towards the field and back again, as if to say, 'You follow me.'

So the men jumped on to their horses and followed the dog, who led them through field after field till they came to a deep hollow in the ground. And there at the bottom they found the little boy fast asleep, with his head pillowed on Toby's side.

They carried him home, still fast asleep, to where his mother was waiting. Soon he was better, and able to tell them what had happened. He had fallen down the hole, and its sides had been too steep for him to climb out, though the dogs had tried to help him. Each night they cuddled close to him and kept him warm; and at last Tom had the idea to go for help, and so it was that he led them to the place where the faithful Toby was watching over his sleeping little friend.

You can imagine what a fuss was made of Tom and Toby, and how they were loved and cared for at the farm, and how they were the little boy's friends and companions all their lives.

Retold from a story in Skipper, My Chum
by Lionel B. Fletcher (Lutterworth Press, 1935).

POLLY AND THE PANSIES

Peter and Polly both had gardens. Peter worked hard in his garden, and it was beautiful. There were no weeds in it, and no stones, and in the middle of it he had a fine bed of pansies. But Polly never did anything in her garden, and it was full of weeds and covered with stones. Her daddy said he would help her to make it tidy, and plant some seeds for her, if she would work too. But Polly just didn't do anything.

All the same, she wished she had a pretty garden, like Peter's. One day the children's uncle Jim came to see them, and Peter showed him his garden. 'It's a splendid garden,' said Uncle Jim. Then he looked at Polly's garden. But he couldn't say that that was splendid too. Then he and Peter went indoors. But Polly stayed behind. She had become very jealous of Peter and his garden. 'Silly old garden!' she said, and she gave a kick at the pansy bed. When she looked, there was a bare patch, and some of the pansies were lying on the path.

Just then her mother came by, and saw what had happened. 'Why, Polly!' she said. 'Whatever has happened to Peter's garden?' Then Polly began to cry and ran to her mother.

'I kicked them,' she said, 'I kicked Peter's pansies. Oh, what shall I do?'

Her mother knelt down. 'What a funny thing to do!' she said. 'Never mind—we'll dig them in again quickly, and they won't come to any harm if we give them a little drink.' She went and fetched a can of water and showed Polly how to water the pansies. Now they were all safely back in the flower bed, and all their funny little faces smiling up at the sun once more.

'Why did you do it, darling?' her mother asked when they had finished. Polly began to cry again. 'I want a nice garden too,' she sobbed, 'and I don't know how to make one.'

'I'll help you,' said her mother. So they went over to Polly's garden. 'First,' said her mother, 'we must pull up all the weeds and clear away the stones. Then you shall see what we will do.' So they made the garden all neat and tidy, and then Polly's mother took her to a shop which sold plants, and there were rows of pansies growing in boxes. Her mother bought a box of pansies, and they took them home and planted them in Polly's garden.

When Father came home, he said, 'Why, Polly, you have some pansies in your garden too.'

'Yes,' said Polly, 'Mummy bought them.'

'Polly helped too,' said her mother. 'We both worked together to get the garden ready for them. And she is going to look after her garden now, aren't you, Polly?'

'Yes, Mummy,' said Polly.

'Polly will be a real gardener some day,' said her mummy.

A LITTLE DOG LOST

Peter had a little white dog called Frisky. He and Peter loved each other very much, and they always did things together. So when Peter went for a holiday in the country with his family, of course Frisky went too.

Frisky loved it in the country. Best of all he loved chasing the rabbits. There were no rabbits in the town where he and Peter lived, and he found it very exciting to have them bob up under his nose and go running away. Off he would rush after them, but he never caught any, because he was so excited that he kept giving short little squeaky barks all the time as he ran, and so, of course, the rabbits could hear him coming and easily get away.

One day Peter and his mummy and daddy, and Frisky too, of course, went for a picnic. They walked through some woods near the house where they were staying, and out into a big field where they had their picnic. After the picnic they all had a rest, and after that they had some marvellous games with a ball in the field. And then they walked back home through the woods again. And all the time Frisky was running here and there and everywhere, sniffing and scratching and looking for those rabbits.

But just when they were nearly home, Peter said, 'Where's Frisky?' They stopped and looked, but he wasn't there. They called and called—'Frisky! Frisky!', but no little dog came running.

'Perhaps he has gone home,' said Peter's mummy. So they went home. But Frisky wasn't there.

'I expect he's gone off on a rabbit hunt by himself,' said Peter's daddy, 'and he'll be back after tea.' So they had their tea. But after tea there was still no Frisky. Peter began to be dreadfully worried.

'I'll go and look for him,' said Peter's daddy.

'Oh, please, can I come too?' begged Peter. 'Please, please!'

'All right,' said his daddy. 'We'll go back the way we came this afternoon, and we'll keep calling as we go.' So he and Peter set out.

When they came to the woods, Peter said, 'The last time I saw him, he was running along by that bank of earth there.' So they walked along by the bank, looking and calling. But there was no Frisky. Peter's daddy was just saying, 'Well, he isn't here——' when Peter called out, 'Listen!'

'I can't hear anything,' said his daddy.

'Yes, listen!' cried Peter. 'I can hear him barking.' They both held their breath and listened, and—yes—there was a faint little bark. It seemed to come from right underneath them.

'He's there! He's there!' cried Peter. 'Look, Daddy, there's a hole—he must be down there.'

'I expect he ran in after a rabbit and got stuck,' said Peter's daddy. 'We must go back and get a spade to dig him out.'

'Oh, Daddy,' said Peter, 'please may I stay here and keep him company?'

'All right,' said his daddy. 'I'll be as quick as I can.'

So he went off, and Peter knelt down by the hole and he kept calling, 'It's all right, Frisky boy. I'm here. Daddy's gone to get a spade, and he's coming back to dig you out. And I'll stay here till he comes. It's all right, Frisky.' And every now and then Frisky would give a feeble little bark underground to show that he understood.

At last Peter's daddy came with the spade and began to dig. He dug and he dug and he *dug*, until at last he put the spade aside and put his arm right down into the earth of the bank and pulled out—not a little white dog, but a little brown dog! It was Frisky, all covered with earth. Frisky shook himself, and then he gave a great big sneeze, and then Peter got hold of him and held him tight, as if he would never let him go. He was so glad to get his little dog back.

Peter carried Frisky home, and the first thing he had was a great big bowl of water. He drank and he drank and he *drank*, because he was so thirsty. And then he had a good dinner, and after that he forgot all about that dreadful time when he was buried in the dark hole in the bank, and was all ready to start chasing rabbits again. But Peter's mummy said, 'Bedtime!'

And when Peter's daddy came to say good night to Peter, he said, 'You know, Peter, you were really the one who rescued Frisky. It was you who thought of looking in the bank, and it was your sharp ears that heard him barking. We might never have found him without your help.'

And when he heard that, Peter was very glad.

THE KIND CAPTAIN

There was once a ferry-boat which carried people and things from one side of a wide river to the other. All sorts of people used the boat—workmen going home, mothers crossing the river to do their shopping, young people going on outings, and children. The ferry-boat had a captain who knew many of these people as friends. But the captain was sad, because the ferry-boat did not make enough money, and he was afraid that the people to whom it belonged might sail it away. And then how would the people cross the river?

One day the captain took the boat out to cross to the other side. Everybody on it was in a hurry to get over. The captain began to steer the boat away from the quay, when a little old lady came hurrying down to the waterside waving her arms. She wanted to come on board.

What should the captain do? Should he go on home to his wife and his supper, or go back for the old lady? He decided to take the old lady on board. But when the passengers saw the boat move back towards the quay, they were annoyed. Why should they have to wait for an old woman? The sailors put down a wooden board and helped the grateful old lady on to the boat.

At the other side of the river, everyone went ashore, and the old lady thanked the captain for his thoughtfulness. Then, when she arrived home, she told her son how kind the captain had been to her. Her son was pleased with the captain and the ferry-boat. He was a businessman, and he arranged for the boat every day to carry large supplies of things to sell from one side of the river to the other. Now, the ferry-boat brought in much more money, and no one wanted to take it from the river. When the passengers knew this, they were grateful to the old lady, and happy that they could still cross the river. But the captain was happier than anyone else. For his ferry-boat had been saved.

Juliet Brittain

THE BULLOCKS' HOLIDAY

In some parts of the great hot continent of India, there are no lorries for people to use when they want to move things from place to place. Instead they use bullocks—great beasts something like our bullocks, but with humps on their backs. These bullocks the Indians harness to their carts, and they pull them slowly along, with the wheels creaking and groaning. It takes a long time to reach the place they have set out for, but they get there in the end.

These bullocks work very hard, and go on pulling their carts till they are too old and tired to do it any more. And because of this, their Indian masters love these faithful servants very much; and one day in every year is set aside for their holiday. On that day they do no work. Their masters take them out and give them a bath; then garlands of flowers are hung round their necks, and they are put into a cattle pen. All the people come together to tell them how much they love them; and they sing a sort of song which goes something like this: 'Oh, bullock, you are wise and good. You are a good worker, and from your labours we have filled our stomachs with food. Today is your holiday; no loads will you draw. Besides, you are going to the town with us, and you will share in the music and dancing that is to take place in your honour. So all the world will know you are a faithful servant.'

After that there is a great procession through the town. All the people take part in it, and every now and again they stop to dance. Some of them carry bells fixed on sticks, and one man plays a drum. And behind them all come the bullocks, walking slowly along with the gay flowers round their necks, and perhaps wondering what it is all about, but very glad not to have to wear their yokes and pull the heavy carts. And that is what happens every year in India on the day which is called the Bullocks' Festival.

> *Based on material from* The Golden Pathway,
> *Vol. II (International University Society).*

WHO THREW THE STONES?

A true story

There was trouble in the school. Someone had been throwing stones, and nobody would own up to having done it. The most likely people seemed to be Jimmy Smith and Peter Jones; but both boys said that they had not done it.

And then the trouble began to spread outside the school. Mrs. Smith said, 'It wasn't my Jimmy. I believe him when he says he didn't do it. It must have been that Peter.' And Mrs. Jones said, 'My Peter didn't do it. It must have been Jimmy.' So they quarrelled, and the trouble got bigger and bigger.

Then one day, in Scripture lesson, the teacher told a story. It was about a man who owed a lot of money to another man, and this man forgave him his debt, so that he didn't have to pay. But this man who had been forgiven such a big debt wouldn't forgive another man who owed him ever such a little money. The teacher said that children, and grown-ups too, often have to say they are sorry for things they have done wrong; and she said that we must not be like the man in the story, but we must forgive other people when they do wrong to us.

The school was a little village school, and on that day the teacher had the big children and the little children all together; and she was really talking to the big ones. She didn't think the little ones would understand. Then she gave out some paper, and told the children to draw someone doing something that he would have to say he was sorry for afterwards.

Most of the big boys drew bank robbers or burglars, and some of the big girls drew someone breaking a doll or a vase or making things untidy. The little ones just scribbled things that nobody else could understand. But Peter Jones, who was only five, had drawn what looked like a scarecrow in a snowstorm.

'What is your picture about?' asked the teacher. 'What are those dots all over it?'

'That's all dirt,' said Peter. 'I threw dirt *and* stones.'

So the teacher said, 'And are you sorry now?'

'Yes,' said Peter. 'I was sorry before, but I thought Mummy was going to smack me, so I said I didn't do it.'

'Well, if you are sorry,' said the teacher, 'why not tell Jimmy so now? You let him be blamed for what you did wrong, you know. There he is, just behind you.'

So Peter turned round and said to Jimmy, 'I'm sorry I threw dirt and stones.' And then they both laughed.

Margaret Sanders

THE KIND MAN AND THE STUPID LITTLE HARE

A true story

A man who loved all animals was once driving along a narrow country road. It was rather a dangerous road, because although on one side there were fields, on the other side was a muddy swamp, and if anyone fell into it he might sink and be suffocated in the mud. As the man passed, he saw in the field there were cattle grazing, and also a little hare nibbling away at the grass. The hare looked up and saw him passing and tried to run away; but instead of running away from the man, it ran towards him! It was so frightened that it became stupid. It ran across the road in front of the car, and then leapt straight into the swamp with a fearful splash.

The man stopped his car, wondering what would happen to the little hare. Would it sink and be swallowed up, or would it find a way out? He could hear splashing in water he could not see, because it was hidden by the marsh grass which covered the swamp; so he got out of his car, climbed over the fence and went down into the marsh. It was very wet and muddy, and his feet sank in over his shoes. Then he saw that the marsh grass was waving about over the place where he had heard the splashing. It kept on moving about —the little hare must still be there. What should he do? If he went any farther, he might sink in and not be able to get out. And yet he could not leave the hare to die.

Then he had an idea. He went back to the car and fetched the handle which can be used for starting it if the self-starter will not work. Then back he went to the swamp. He could see the little hare now. It had struggled towards the edge of the swamp, but he could see that it was so tired that it could not go much farther. He hooked the handle round the hare and pulled it towards him till he could lift it out. He waded back to the bank, climbed over the fence and put the little hare down on the road.

And then—would you believe it? That stupid little hare

jumped straight back into the swamp! It must have been just too frightened to think where it was. And so the man had to set to work to rescue it all over again. This time, when he had caught it, he put it in his car and drove up to higher ground where there was dry land on both sides. And then at last the kind man picked up the poor wet shivering little animal and let it hop away to safety.

Retold from a story in Sunday Express
by Thurlow Craig, 23 October 1966.

HOW JOHNNY SAVED THE TRAIN

A true story

Many years ago, in America, there lived a little boy called Johnny Tomkins. Johnny's father was a guard on the railway. One day Johnny went to meet his father at the station. The train came in, and there was his father's face looking at him out of the guard's van.

'Jump in, Johnny,' said his father. 'I have certain things to attend to on the train, so you wait here for me. Then we will go home.'

So off went Johnny's father along the train, and Johnny waited in the guard's van. Now this train had come to the end of its journey, and was to stay in the station all night. The guard's van was in the end carriage of the train, and, unknown to Johnny and his father, someone had unfastened this last carriage from the train, perhaps to join it on to another train. It happened that the engine at the front of the train shunted back a little, and this started the end carriage moving. At first it went very slowly, but the line was slightly downhill, and it began to go faster and faster. Johnny looked out of the window, and saw that it was running away, with only him inside it.

Presently it turned a bend in the line; and then Johnny's heart gave a big bump with fear, for far down the line he could see a red light, and he knew that it was the light on the engine of an express train. It was coming on at full speed, and soon the runaway carriage would crash into it, and there would be a terrible accident.

Johnny felt very frightened, not only for himself but for all the people travelling on the express train. And then he remembered something his mother had said. She had said that even children, if they keep their heads, and really try, and ask God to help them, can do great things in the world. So Johnny knelt down on the floor of the guard's van and asked God to help him save the train.

When he stood up, he felt much braver, and an idea came into his head. In those days guards carried red lanterns, and his father's lantern stood lighted near the stove. He picked it up and ran out on to the little platform which is on the end of American railway carriages. Then he waved the lantern up and down as hard as he could. The driver on the engine down below saw the flashing light, and knew that a red light meant danger. At once he put on the brakes, and slowly the great train came to a stop, slowly it moved backwards, and then, just as the runaway carriage reached it, it came to a side-line and swung off along it. The train and all the passengers on it were safe.

The train came to a stop, and all the passengers jumped out to see what had happened. When they found out what Johnny had done, they were so grateful to him for saving their lives that they collected money for a present for him. Johnny was pleased to have it; but he was still more pleased that God had answered his prayer and helped him to save the train.

THE FAITHFUL WATCHDOG

A true story

This is the story of a man who lived in a far-off country, which is called Indonesia, and of his little dog Chu. The man is telling the story himself, and this is what he says:

In the tropical heat of Medan everyone sleeps with open windows, and almost all the houses are of the bungalow type. . . . When going to bed I was in the habit of hanging my clothes on a chair near the open window, and I very often forgot to take my wallet and my money out of the pockets. One night I was suddenly awakened by Chu's furious barking. When I got up I found him scratching at my bedroom door, asking to be let in. Suddenly I saw a long bamboo pole sticking into the room through a hole in the wire netting which screened the window. The burglar had carefully cut this hole, then he had fished my jacket off the chair with his pole, complete with wallet and loose change, right out through the window; but when Chu had woken up and barked he had dropped my trousers on to the window-sill—and fled.

(My servants) Meenah and Mohammed, in their white nightshirts, like white ghosts with dark faces, arrived breathlessly. Chu barked furiously, and wanted to lead me out of the front gate into the dark night. We went all round the house, but, of course, there was nobody to be seen at that time. I was sorry to lose my wallet, naturally, but I was very sleepy, and, in any case, there was not much we could do except telephone the police. They said they would have a good look round in the morning . . . so we all went back to sleep.

Because of all the excitement I awoke with a headache very early the next morning. In order to take some exercise while it was still cool, I whistled for Chu, and together we walked through the Chinese street next to our garden. Suddenly the dog let out a yell and flew at the throat of a tall Chinese youth who was passing us. His yellow face became white with fright; he looked wildly round, then broke into a run, with Chu at his heels. This was strange, as Chu never barked at . . . neighbours. . . . I started to run too, trying to call Chu off. The youth jumped over a ditch, climbed a fence, and in doing so dropped a small parcel, which Chu brought to me in his teeth. It was my wallet, tied up in a few rags. Chu had recognised the burglar of the night before by his smell! A policeman arrived from nowhere, somebody else helped to give chase . . . and the youth was promptly caught.

Chu was very proud. I was afraid his tail might drop off, he wagged it so hard. You can imagine what a good meal Meenah gave him when he got home. Everyone in town heard the story, and during all the years we lived in the old house we never had another burglar.'

From A Zoo of My Own *by Cornelius Conyn* (*Harrap, 1957*).

JUDY AND THE TELEPHONE

Based on a true story

Judy often wished she could use the telephone. Once or twice she had spoken to her daddy on it, but she had never rung anyone up all by herself.

'Mummy,' she said one day, 'may I ring up somebody on the phone?'

'Phones are for grown-ups,' said her mother. 'They're not to play about with.'

'But I want to phone somebody up. Oh, can't I, please?' begged Judy.

'Well, who could you phone?'

'My friend Wendy at school has the phone,' said Judy.

'I suppose you could ring Wendy and ask her to tea,' said her mother.

'Oh yes, do let me ask her,' cried Judy. 'How shall I do it?'

'Well, you have to know her number first,' said her mother, 'and that would be in the telephone directory. If you could read, you could find it yourself; but it is rather hard, so I'll do it for you.'

So they looked in the directory and found the number.

Judy was able to dial it, because she knew how to read numbers. And soon she heard a 'Br-br' noise in her ear.

'This is Mrs. Adams speaking,' said a voice. 'Who is that?'

'It's Judy. Can Wendy come to tea with me?'

'Oh, hello, Judy,' said Mrs. Adams. 'I'm sure Wendy would love to come to tea with you. What day would you like her to come?'

'Ask her for tomorrow,' said Judy's mother. So Judy said, 'Tomorrow.'

'Yes, she could come then,' said Wendy's mother. 'Would you like to speak to her? Wendy!' Judy could hear her calling, and soon Wendy said, 'Hullo, Judy.'

'Hullo, Wendy.'

'I'll see you tomorrow,' was the last thing Wendy said. Judy was quite excited when she put down the phone. It was fun to do something new, and she felt very big. The next day she helped her mother make some cakes, and when Wendy came they had a lovely tea and then went to play in the garden with Spotty, Judy's dog.

'I am just going down the road now,' said Judy's mummy, 'to post a letter, but I won't be long.' And off she went.

But while she was away, a very nasty thing happened. Spotty was running after a ball when it went into a rubbish heap. Spotty went in after it. Then he gave a loud yelp and came limping back to them, with his paw bleeding badly.

The children didn't know what to do. He wouldn't let them touch the bad paw, and growled when they tried. Suddenly, Judy had an idea. 'Let's ring up your mummy and tell her,' she said to Wendy. 'Quick! Then she'll tell us what to do.'

'Do you know how?' asked Wendy. 'I don't know our number.' 'I do, though,' said Judy. And she rang up and got the number.

When Mrs. Adams answered it, she was surprised to hear Judy speaking. 'Why, your mother's here,' she said. 'She was passing, so she called in to ask if I would like to come and sit in your garden till it is time to take Wendy home. Here she is now.'

'Hullo, Judy,' said her mother. 'Whatever——' But Judy didn't wait for her to finish. 'Oh, Mummy, come quick, please,' she cried. 'Spotty's hurt his paw, and it's bleeding dreadfully. Do come!'

'Of course, dear,' said her mother. 'Don't go near him—he might bite you if he's hurt. I'm coming.'

It was only a few minutes until Mummy came, but it seemed like years to Judy and Wendy. When she came, she put a bandage round Spotty's mouth to stop him biting, then she had a good look at his paw, washed it and bound it up.

'My goodness,' she said at last, 'it's stopped bleeding now, but if he had been left much longer, he might have been very ill. He must have cut his paw on some broken glass. Fancy that happening, just the minute I left you! You were a sensible girl, Judy, to think of ringing up Mrs. Adams.'

Margaret Sanders

SOMETHING SPECIAL FOR KATE

A true story

There was once a little girl called Kate who lived with her mummy and her daddy. They had FUN. Even when she was only a tiny baby, she went everywhere with them in her carry-cot in the back of the car. When they went to parties, she went too, and slept all the time on someone's bed. Then, as she grew older, she often sat on her mother's knee in the front of the car.

When summer time came, they had lovely holidays. One summer they drove all the way to Spain. Every night, when they got out of the car, they put up a little blue tent and slept inside it. When at last they got there, there were golden beaches to play on and warm sea splashing up on them to bathe in. Kate paddled and built sand castles and played ball with Daddy, while Mummy lay in the sun and got brown. They were as happy as three people could be.

Then one day, as Kate and her mother were washing up the tea-things together, Kate's mother said, 'Katie, I've got something nice to tell you.'

'Hooray!' cried Kate. 'Are we going off with the little blue tent again?' That was the nicest thing she could think of.

'Oh no,' said her mother. 'It's something exciting in quite a different way.'

'Oh, Mummy, *do* tell me.'

'Well, I wonder what you'll think when you hear that we're going to have a little new baby.'

Kate was most surprised. She had thought they would always be just Daddy and Mummy and Kate.

'But it will be *your* baby,' went on Mummy, 'for you will help Daddy and me to look after it.'

'Is it coming today?' asked Kate.

'Oh no, not for a few weeks. But there's a lot of planning that we must do to get ready for it. The first thing is to buy some clothes.'

So Kate and her mother went shopping, and bought some nightgowns and a pretty pale yellow blanket. Then Daddy said, 'Now you're such a big girl, I think you need a new bed.' So one Saturday afternoon Mummy and Daddy and Kate chose a proper grown-up bed for Kate. She was thrilled.

Then Mummy said, 'Now we must think and plan how you can help me with the baby. I shall need a lot of help at bathing time.'

'I know!' said Kate. 'I'll hold the sponge, and when you say "Squeeze!", I'll squeeze it and trickle the water from it over the baby to wash the soap away.'

'That's a good idea,' said her mother. 'And why don't we put the nappies and the nightgowns in this low drawer?

Then I'll say, "Nappy, please," and you'll run and fetch it for me.' So they planned for the new baby.

The time went quite quickly, till at last one morning early, Mummy went away to hospital and Granny came to stay. That evening the telephone rang, and Kate rushed to answer it. It was Daddy.

'Kate,' he said, 'your little baby has arrived, and she's a girl. What do you think of that?'

Kate was glad to hear the news, but what she wanted to know was, 'When is Mummy coming home?'

'Not for a few days; but here she is on the telephone,' said Daddy. Sure enough, there was Mummy's voice on the line, and she and Kate had a great chat.

Every evening after that Kate telephoned to her mother and heard the news of the new baby. And every evening she asked, 'When are you coming home?'

At last Mummy said, 'I'll be home tomorrow.' And sure enough, the next day Daddy drove up with the car and Mummy got out. Kate rushed into her arms and they had a good hug. Then Daddy lifted the carry-cot very carefully off the back seat. Inside it Kate could just see a tiny face, almost hidden by a shawl.

They came into the house, laughing and joking, while the baby slept. When they had finished tea, she woke up. Then Mummy sat Kate on a stool and put the new baby into her arms.

'There's your baby, Kate,' she said. 'What do you think of her?'

Kate felt bursting with pride as she held her.

'My baby's lovely,' she said. 'And when we go out in the car, *she'll* be in the back now.'

'And you'll be in the front with us,' said Daddy. 'You'll see—we'll have more fun than ever before, because now we'll be four instead of only three.'

Rosalie Procter

JOHN AND THE BIG DOG

Based on a true story

John was only a small boy, but he had a big plan—he wanted to be a sailor when he grew up. He had a game about the sea which he liked to play in the sitting-room. He pretended the floor was all water, and the mats were islands. The chairs were houses on the islands, and you had to sit on an old stool for a boat, and row it on the water with your legs. If anyone came into the room, John would call out, 'Mind the boat! You mustn't tread there, or you'll get wet!' His mother had quite a job to get to the cupboard without stepping in the wrong places; but she didn't mind, because she knew about John wanting to be a sailor.

Most mornings he played boats, and in the afternoons he usually went for a walk to the shops with his mother. He enjoyed looking at the shops, and the men working on the road, and all the cars and lorries going by. But there was one road he didn't enjoy going up, and that was his own road, where he lived. In fact, he hated it, and he sometimes didn't want to go out at all, he hated it so much. And it was all because of a big dog that lived on the corner at the end of the road. This dog sat in the gateway, and when anyone went past, he stretched out his great black head and curled his lips back so that you could see all his teeth, and growled and barked till you were out of sight. Everyone said he was not a fierce dog, and would never bite anyone; but John didn't believe that, because of the frightening noises he made. So one day John's daddy called at the house where the dog lived and asked the people if they would mind keeping the gate shut, so that John wouldn't be frightened; and they did that. But then John was afraid that the dog would jump over the gate, and every day he got more and more worried, until at last he screamed every time his mother wanted to take him up the road.

His mother and father thought a lot about how they could

help him not to be afraid. And one day his father came home with a beautiful new book about ships and the sea. It had pictures of ships in harbour, ships far out at sea, barges on the canals, yacht races and at the end a splendid picture of a lifeboat going out in a storm. Daddy said that if John went to bed early, he would read the book to him in bed. So John hurried up with his washing, gave his teeth a quick brush and jumped into bed. Daddy sat on the bed, and they looked at the book together.

'I'd like to go in that big ship,' John said, as they turned the pages. And when they came to the last picture, the lifeboat, he said, 'I'd be brave like those men. I'd go out in the lifeboat if the big ships were sinking.'

'Would you?' said Daddy. 'Wouldn't you be frightened of the big waves?'

'Sailors aren't frightened,' said John.

'Well,' said Daddy, 'they are sometimes; but even if they are, they still have to carry on, and not stop to think how they feel. Brave people do often feel frightened, just like other people, but they go on all the same.'

John thought a lot about what his daddy had said. Next day, when his mummy wanted to go shopping, she said to John, 'Will you come to the shops with me today, or would you rather stay next door till I come back?' And John said, 'I want to come with you.'

So they set out along the road towards the corner where the big dog lived. When they got near the dog's house and he started barking, John began to feel very shaky; but he hurried past and tried not to look at him. Once he had got past, he felt quite pleased with himself, and he thought, 'I needn't have worried really. He only makes a noise—he doesn't come out.'

That night his daddy looked at the book with him again. They looked for a long time at the lifeboat picture. Then John said, 'The lifeboat men go out, don't they, even if they are just a teeny bit frightened?'

'It's easier to be brave if you are big,' said Daddy. 'But if you practise now on the little things, when you are big you'll be the bravest sailor on the sea.'

John thought for a while, then he said, 'When I'm a sailor, I mustn't be afraid of bigger things than dogs.' I know what he meant—don't you?

Margaret Sanders

STEPHEN'S MEDAL

There was once a family who went to the seaside for a holiday. There were Daddy and Mummy and Auntie and Stephen. Stephen wasn't very big.

They drove to the seaside by car, and got there a little before tea. The place where they were staying was a nice little house with a garden, which some friends had lent them. It was quite near the sea, and they went down to have a look at it before tea. Stephen hadn't seen the sea before, and he wasn't sure that he liked it. The waves kept coming right up to his feet. But he found that if he stood still they always went away again; so then he wasn't frightened any more.

After they had had their tea, Mummy said, 'Now, how are we going to divide up all the jobs there are to do? I shall do the cooking'.

'I'll do the shopping and clean the house,' said Auntie.

'And I'll do the odd jobs in the garden,' said Daddy.

'And what shall I do?' asked Stephen.

His mother thought for a bit. 'You can be the milk-bottle-putter-outer,' she said at last.

'What is that?' asked Stephen. It sounded very important.

'It's quite easy,' said Mummy. 'Look—I'll show you.' She took the milk bottle and emptied all the milk that was left in it into a jug. Then she washed and dried it and gave it to Stephen.

'Now come outside the back door,' she said. And she showed him something he had never seen before. It was like a little tray with wires on top that made round holes. And it was painted blue. 'Put the bottle into one of the holes,' said Mummy. So Stephen did, and it just fitted nicely.

'I'll order more milk for tomorrow,' said Mummy, 'and that will mean more bottles for you to put out.'

After that they each did their jobs every day. Mummy cooked lovely meals; and Auntie kept the house as neat as a new pin, and took Stephen out with her when she went to the shops; Daddy made the garden beautifully neat and tidy, and Stephen helped with that too. And every night before he went to bed he did his special job, and put out the milk bottles. Sometimes there were two bottles, and sometimes there were three, and once there were visitors, and Mummy had to get extra milk, and that night there were four bottles to be put out.

It was a lovely holiday. When he got used to the sea, Stephen wanted to be beside it as much as he could, and they went down to the beach every day. It was such fun to have the sea at the bottom of the garden.

When Auntie and Stephen went to the shops, they bought Stephen a bright blue bucket and a wooden spade. And when they went down to the beach that afternoon, Daddy showed Stephen how to make sand castles. You had to fill the bucket full of sand—quite, quite full—and then smack it down with the spade till it was flat on top. Then you turned it over, and gave it a little shake, and out came a beautiful little sand castle, just the same shape as the bucket, only the other way up.

'Now let me try,' said Stephen, after Daddy had made several sand castles. He filled the bucket with sand, and smacked the top down flat; and then he turned it over. But oh dear!—what came out was not a beautiful little sand castle, but a muddly mess of sand. Stephen was very disappointed.

'You didn't fill it full enough,' said Daddy, 'and you didn't pat it down hard enough. Look, I'll show you again.'

He made another sand castle, and then Stephen tried once more; and this time his sand castle came out just as good as Daddy's. Stephen *was* pleased! He went on making sand castles one after the other, and by the time he had to go in to bed he had made a whole round ring of them.

Next morning after breakfast he ran down to the sea shore to see his sand castles again. But they were all gone!

'The tide has washed them away,' said Daddy. 'Never mind, Stephen—we can easily make some more.'

They did lots of other exciting things on their holiday too. They bathed and paddled and played games on the beach, and they had lots of picnics, and they went out in a boat. But then at last the end of their holiday came, and it was time to go home. The night before they were to start, Stephen put out his last milk bottles in the blue wire stand.

Next morning, when Stephen came down to breakfast, Daddy said, 'Look, Stephen, there's something beside your plate.' And there he saw something big and round and shining with letters on it.

'What is it?' he asked.

'It's a medal,' Daddy said, 'a milk-bottle-putter-outer's medal. See those letters—M.B.P.O.—? They stand for Milk-Bottle-Putter-Outer.'

'Is it for me?' asked Stephen.

'Yes,' said Daddy. 'I made it specially for you—it's to show that you are the champion milk-bottle-putter-outer.' And he pinned the big shiny medal on to Stephen's jersey.

Stephen was very proud of his medal, and he wore it all the way home in the car, to show how he had helped on the holiday.

TRUCKS AND DIESELS

Based on a true story

This story is about two boys named Malcolm and Desmond and some of their friends. They were in the same class at school, and they lived near a big railway station. Whenever they had a holiday from school, they would go down to the station and watch the trains.

They liked school, especially when the class made models of things like stations or aerodromes. One day they were all working on a model of a castle. The towers were made of tea boxes, and the walls of cornflakes packets, and it was all stuck together with strong glue. All the children in the group worked hard, except one, who was called Tommy. Tommy was supposed to paint the walls; but instead of mixing the paint, he found a comic to read. Desmond took it away from him and made him get on with the mixing—he wanted to finish the castle. When Tommy had done some painting, he went to wash his hands; but he was a long time because he was playing with the water. The other children kept working, but Tommy wouldn't bother. He was a lazy boy.

At last Desmond, who was leader of the group, went to the teacher and said, 'Need we have Tommy in our group? He won't work.' So teacher made Tommy copy some writing about castles; and he had to do it all through playtime, because he was so slow.

Malcolm helped with the painting, and kept on till it was all finished. While they were working, he said to Desmond, 'How many diesels did you spot last night?'

'Only five,' said Desmond. 'They were mostly trucks.'

'I don't like trucks,' said Malcolm. 'Too slow.'

'Hey,' said Desmond, 'don't you think Tommy's like a truck? He won't work on his own—always has to be pushed or pulled, like a truck.'

'Yes—and you're like a diesel,' said Malcolm. 'You've sort of got an engine of your own, and you pull other people along with you.'

Just then the teacher came round to see how they were getting on.

'Please, miss,' said Malcolm, 'I've just had a good idea. Tommy's a truck and Desmond's a diesel.'

'Whatever do you mean by that?' asked the teacher.

'Why, Desmond does things by himself, but Tommy has to be pushed and pulled by somebody else.'

'Not a bad idea,' she said. 'I wish you were all diesels, then.'

Next morning they were doing sums. Desmond said to Malcolm, 'I'm going to see if I can get a row of ticks right down the page.'

'Good for you, diesel,' said Malcolm, 'I bet I do more than you.' Then they both worked away as hard as they could.

In a few days, the whole school had got hold of the idea of trucks and diesels. When Tommy started rolling his pencil down the desk instead of working, the teacher said, 'Now, Tommy, see if you can be a diesel instead of a truck.' Then one day she showed the children some badges with coloured pictures of diesels on them.

'Coo! I'd like one of those!' said Tommy.

'You can have one,' said the teacher, 'when you've learnt to work on your own.' Then she gave out the badges. Not all the children had them. Tommy didn't. When he got home, he said to his mother, 'All the children were given badges today except me.' Which wasn't quite true, was it? But Tommy wasn't particular about telling the truth unless it suited him.

His mother said, 'Why didn't you get one?'

'I don't know,' said Tommy. (But he did really, didn't he?)

Then Tommy's mother thought to herself, 'I'll see that that teacher treats my Tommy fairly. I'll go and talk to her.' And she did. 'Why didn't my Tommy get a badge like all the others?' she asked.

So then the teacher told her what the badge was for, and why Tommy didn't get one.

'I'm afraid he is a naughty boy at home too,' said his mother. 'He won't go to bed when I tell him, for one thing.'

'If he's too tired, of course he can't work,' said the teacher.

So they talked to Tommy, and told him what he must do to get a badge. And he did try. When it was time for bed, he said, 'Let me stay up a bit longer. I want to watch this on television.'

'You won't get your badge if you're tired,' said his mother.

'I don't care,' said Tommy.

'Yes, you do care,' said his mother. 'Come on now.' Then he came.

Then one day at school the teacher told the children about coral, the beautiful coloured hard stuff made by creatures under the sea; and she showed them some pictures taken right under the water.

'I've seen that on television,' said Tommy.

'Have you?' said teacher. 'Perhaps you would paint us a picture of it.'

Tommy painted a really good picture. He worked hard; he put in coral and striped fishes and frogmen with cameras. He made it look really watery, with blue and green and white paint. It was the best thing he had ever done. Everyone said so, and it was put on the wall right by the door. A visitor came one day, and said, 'Who painted that lovely picture?'

Tommy was very proud. He knew it was good, and that he had done his best. He felt all warm inside. He thought, 'I will try again.'

The next model the children made was a farm. Desmond and Malcolm made the farmhouse, and other children wanted to make the animals. Teacher said, 'Who will paint the background?'

Then Desmond said, 'Please, can we have Tommy, because he is such a good painter?'

'Yes,' said the teacher. 'I am sure Tommy will do it well. He did such a good picture of the sea.'

Tommy was very pleased. This time, too, he worked hard and did his best.

Malcolm said, 'Tommy's a diesel now. I think he's got his own engine at last.'

By the end of term, Tommy had actually won a diesel badge. He was not quite as good as some of the children, but he had done so much better that the teacher gave it to him.

'Keep it up!' she said, as she pinned it on. 'Now you have an engine of your own. You are not a truck any more.'

Margaret Sanders

II

STORIES OF FANTASY

THE LITTLE RED HEN

The little red hen was in the farmyard with her chickens, when she found a grain of wheat.

'Who will plant this wheat?' she said.

'Not I,' said the goose.

'Not I,' said the duck.

'I will, then,' said the little red hen; and she planted the grain of wheat.

When the wheat was ripe, she said, 'Who will take this wheat to the mill?'

'Not I,' said the goose.

'Not I,' said the duck.

'I will, then,' said the little red hen; and she took the wheat to the mill.

When she brought the flour home, she said, 'Who will make some bread with this flour?'

'Not I,' said the goose.

'Not I,' said the duck.

'I will, then,' said the little red hen.

When the bread was baked, she said, 'Who will eat this bread?'

'I will,' said the goose.

'I will,' said the duck.

'No, you won't,' said the little red hen. 'I shall eat it myself. Cluck! Cluck!' And she called her chickens to help her.

BIG BLACK BOUNCER

There was once a rabbit. He was a big rabbit, and he was a black rabbit, and his name was Bouncer. The other animals in the wood called him Big Black Bouncer, and they didn't like him at all.

You see, he thought he was bigger and cleverer than all the other animals, and he was always laughing at them and making fun of them.

'You silly little squirrel!' he would say. 'You can't jump in the air like me.' And he would make a mighty spring right up into the air. (That's why he was called Bouncer.)

Or he would see a tiny mouse hiding in the grass, and he would call out, 'You miserable little mouse, you can't dig big holes in the ground like me.' And he would scrape and scratch at the earth with his strong hind legs till he had made a really *huge* hole.

And when he saw a frog hopping by, he would laugh and say, 'You foolish frog, you're such a tiny scrap that people would hardly notice you. But just look at me—I'm Big Black Bouncer, and everyone notices *me*!'

But he went on bouncing about, and eating grass and other nice green things, and getting bigger and bigger and fatter and fatter, until one day he tried to dive down a hole he hadn't used for some time. In he went, head first—and there he stuck! He couldn't get out again. He couldn't even call for help, because his nose and mouth were stuck tight in the hole. All he could do was to drum hard with his strong hind legs—dub-a-dub-a-dub-a-dub!

The little mouse heard this strange noise, and came scurrying out to see what it was. Off she ran to tell the squirrel; and the squirrel told the frog, and the frog told the hedgehog, and the hedgehog told the mole; and they all came to look at Big Black Bouncer's legs sticking out of the hole.

'Serves him right,' said the squirrel.

'Let him stay there,' said the frog.

'We don't want him back,' said the hedgehog.

But the little mouse said, 'I feel very sorry for him. I think we ought to help him get out.' So the animals talked it over, and they agreed that they would try to pull Big Black Bouncer out of the hole.

They all caught hold of each other, and the biggest of them caught hold of his legs, and they pulled and they pulled and they *pulled*! How they did pull! And at last there was a big *pop*—and out came Big Black Bouncer.

He sat and looked at all the little animals who had helped him—the squirrel and the frog and the hedgehog and the mole and the teeny, weeny little field mouse.

'Thank you,' said Big Black Bouncer. And then he said, 'I needed you all just now. But it was very kind of you to come and help me when I've been so horrid to you and laughed at you so much. I'm sorry I did it, and I'll never do it again.'

And after that they were all good friends in the wood.

THE KIND LITTLE CAT

Based on a true story

Two animals once lived in a house. One was a big dog called Dinah, and the other was a little cat called Smoky. Dinah and Smoky were very fond of each other. They liked to play together, and to sleep together in front of the fire.

And one day they did something else together. They each had a family. Dinah had four lovely puppies, and Smoky had five tiny kittens. And because they were such good friends, their mistress put Dinah's big basket with the puppies and Smoky's little box with the kittens in the same room together.

One day their mistress took Dinah out for a run, and when they came back she noticed that the big dog was limping along on three legs, and holding up the fourth paw as if it hurt.

'What's the matter with your foot, Dinah?' she asked. 'Let me see.' She took the paw in her hand, and saw that there was something sticking in it and making it sore—

a piece of grit or a thorn. She tried to get whatever it was out, but she couldn't.

'We shall have to go to the vet, Dinah,' she said. So she went and got out the car. 'You must leave your babies for a little while, Dinah,' she said. 'We shan't be long. Hop in.' So Dinah hopped into the car, and off they went.

Smoky, in her box, had just finished feeding her kittens and giving them all a good wash, and now she had settled them all down to sleep. They were very quiet. But the puppies in Dinah's basket were not at all quiet. Their mummy had never gone away for so long before, and they did not like it. 'Mummy,' they cried, 'Mummy, where are you?' It was only a little cry at first, but it got louder and *louder* and LOUDER, till at last they were making a simply tremendous noise.

Smoky in her box felt very sorry for them. 'Poor little darlings!' she thought. 'Their mother really should come back and look after them. I would never leave *my* babies like that.' The puppies cried and cried, and at last Smoky said, 'I must see what I can do. Thank goodness my children are all asleep and quiet.'

So she jumped out of her box and walked softly over to Dinah's basket and jumped in among the puppies. 'Hush! Hush!' she said. 'Don't make so much noise. Your mummy will be back soon. Now lie down and go to sleep like good children.'

The puppies were very surprised to find this little grey furry person in their basket, instead of their big hairy mother. But what she said was very comforting, and after a time they stopped crying and settled down quietly.

'Now I'll sing you the sleepy song I sing to my kittens,' said Smoky. And she sang 'Purr–r–r. Purr–r–r,' ever so softly till all the puppies were asleep like the kittens.

And then Dinah and her mistress came home. The vet had taken the piece of grit out of Dinah's paw and tied it up so that it didn't hurt any more.

'You'd better hurry along to your babies, Dinah,' said her mistress. 'I expect they are hungry, and crying for you.'

They hurried into the room where the box and the basket were. But all was quiet. The five kittens were still fast asleep, and in the basket sat Smoky purring away, with the puppies asleep all round her. But she jumped out of the basket as soon as she saw Dinah.

'Why, Smoky, you kind little cat!' said her mistress. 'You have been looking after Dinah's babies as well as your own!' And Dinah wagged her tail as she got into her basket—that was her way of saying 'Thank you, Smoky' too.

THE KID WHO OBEYED

In a stable lived a goat which had a pretty little kid, of which she was very fond. One day she said to her, 'My dear, I am going to fetch a cabbage and a lettuce for your dinner. Mind you do not go out while I am away. Lock the door of our stable, and do not open it to anyone who knocks, without first looking out of the window to see who it is that wants to come in. Pray, mind what I say to you, and do as I bid you.'

'Yes, Mother,' said the kid. 'Do not be afraid. I will do as you bid.'

So off the old goat went; but she waited outside the door while the little kid shut it, and she looked back very often to see that it was kept shut.

A wolf who lived near saw the goat pass by. He had often wished to eat up that nice tender young kid, and this day, having had no breakfast, he was very hungry. 'Aha! Now that the old mother is out, I will go and eat that silly young kid. She will be sure to leave the door open.' Away he went to the stable where the old goat lived. He went to the door with a bounce, thinking to push it open. . . . But he could not get in.

'Although you have fastened the door, Miss Kid,' growled he to himself, 'I will eat you—I will knock, and you will be sure to come and open the door. And then——' He was so pleased with the thought of eating the little kid that he licked his lips and, lifting up his paw, gave a loud knock at the door.

'Who is there outside?' asked the little kid from inside.

'I, my dear,' said the wolf, trying to speak like the goat, 'I, your mother; open the door quickly; I am in a hurry.'

'Oh no, you cannot be my mother,' said the kid.

'Open the door this minute, or I shall be very angry with you,' said the wolf.

'If you are my mother,' said the little kid, 'you will wait while I open the window, for my mother told me to do so before I opened the door.' . . . So the wise little kid went up to the window and looked out.

'Oh, you bad wolf' said she 'to try to cheat me; but you will not eat me today, so you may go away—ha! ha! ha!', and the kid laughed.

The wolf gnashed his teeth and growled. He looked very fierce at the little kid, but he could not reach her. The kid went from the window, but the wolf still heard her 'Ha! ha! ha!' as she laughed at him safe inside the stable.

The wolf went away, and soon afterwards the goat came back. She knocked at the door. The little kid asked, 'Who is there?'

'It is I, your mother, darling,' said the goat.

'You speak like my mother, but I will be sure,' said the kid, 'before I open the door. If you are my mother really, you will not mind waiting while I look out of the window.'

So again the kid looked out of the window, and when she saw it was her own mother, she ran quickly and opened the door.

'Dear mother,' said she, 'such a large, cruel wolf has been here; but I did as you bid me; I looked out of the window before I opened the door.'

'Dear kid,' said the goat, and she licked her with her tongue, 'good kid, wise little kid! If you had not obeyed me, that cruel, greedy wolf would have eaten you up, and you would never have seen your mother again. Good child, to do as I bid you.'

And then the goat gave the kid the fine lettuce and cabbage she had brought home with her.

From The Children's Story Garden (*J. B. Lippincott Company*). *Slightly shortened.*

BILLY THE GUITAR

Once there was a guitar called Billy who belonged to a girl called Annette. Billy loved it when she played on him to her friends; and he thought it rather a fine thing that they all liked to spend time listening to him.

Then one day Annette took Billy to join some violins, 'cellos, a trumpet, oboes, a piano and other instruments. For they were all going to play a piece of music together, and this music needed a guitar. At first Billy was excited. He really was something big now. But presently he found that, when he played, people couldn't always hear him because all the other instruments made so much noise. So he got sulky.

Billy's place was next to the piano. The piano had taken a liking to Billy, and decided to help him. So when Billy played badly, the piano knew what was the matter.

'I say, Billy,' said the piano, 'don't be unhappy. You may have been trying to give out a beautiful tune when you and Annette played by yourselves; but now we are all trying to make beautiful music together.'

Billy was sorry for being sulky, and spoiling the music. So, from then on, he played well.

The day came when they were all to play in a big concert before some famous foreign visitors. The players arrived, and the people in their lovely clothes sat and talked. Suddenly there was a hush, and everyone stood up. In came an English family—and the famous foreign visitors.

'It's the king and queen of Telemar,' whispered the piano to Billy, 'and they've brought the crown prince and the two princesses with them.'

The king and queen and all the guests sat down, and the instruments began to play. But soon the piano whispered to Billy, 'I don't feel very well. I'm not so young as I used to be, and I think one of my strings is going to lose its voice.'

'Come on,' said Billy, cheering him up, 'we've got to show our friends out there what we can do for them. I'll help you. We'd be lost without you.' So the old piano took heart and played better than ever before.

At last the concert ended. The people and the instruments all agreed that it had been a wonderfully happy evening. Billy was sure that the royal family of Telemar had clapped specially for the piano.

But then he had a surprise. The royal family asked him to play for them all on his own.

'For,' said the queen, 'we have many guitars in our country, and we love the music you play.'

So Billy and Annette played for them, and everyone had a wonderful afternoon.

And ever since, Billy has gone on playing with the orchestra, and enjoyed helping to make people happy.

Juliet Brittain

BIG BEN AND LITTLE BEN

Little Ben was a tiny blue enamel clock, and he lived on the mantelpiece in a little boy's bedroom. The bedroom was in a flat that was quite close to Big Ben, who, as everyone knows, is one of the largest clocks in the world.

Little Ben used to feel very miserable when he heard Big Ben's voice boom out the hours, because *he* had only a tiny little voice like a tinkling silver bell, and he simply longed to be a great big clock with a great big voice that could be heard all over London Town. Poor Little Ben grew so

unhappy that something went wrong with his works. Sometimes he would be half an hour too fast, sometimes he would
be half an hour too slow; and one day the little boy, whose
name was Peter, was late for school, all because Little Ben
was so unhappy.

'We'll have to send him to the clock shop,' said Mummy,
shaking Little Ben gently. 'I'm sure there's something loose
inside.'

'Oh dear,' thought Little Ben, 'I don't want a clock-man
fussing about with my works. Big Ben never has to go to
the clock-shop. Oh dear, oh dear, oh dear, why have I got
to be such a poor wretched little clock?' And he began to
tick and tick in the most alarming manner.

'Yes,' said Mummy, putting him back on the mantelpiece,
'I'll take him to the clock-shop first thing in the morning.'

But that night, when Peter was curled up fast asleep in his
little white bed, and the big round moon was silvering the
roofs of London Town, and Big Ben had just boomed the
last stroke of twelve o'clock, Little Ben heard a squeaky
voice just beside him say, 'Hello, Little Ben; I hear things
are not going too well with you these days.'

And there, perched in a patch of moonlight on the mantelpiece, Little Ben saw the strangest little creature you could
possibly imagine; a tiny little man with a long white beard,
carrying a shining silver sickle over one small shoulder.

'Who are you?' ticked Little Ben in surprise.

'I'm Father Time,' said the little old man, chuckling. 'All
the time in the world belongs to me, and all the clocks in the
world are my servants.'

'But I thought Father Time was a huge old fellow,' ticked
Little Ben.

'Well, I'm *not*, as you can see,' said Father Time, 'but I'm
every bit as important as a giant, for all that. And that's just
what's the matter with you,' he went on, pointing a finger
at Little Ben. 'You think only big people are important,
which is very stupid. You're just as important as Big Ben

over there, because you're *both* my servants. You both strike the same hours, and your hands go round in exactly the same way. So just make up your mind to be happy, knowing that *you're* just as important in *your* place as Big Ben in his. If you're not happy, you won't be able to do your job properly; and you know what clock-menders are. . . .' And with a wave of his hand, Father Time vanished.

Little Ben thought a lot about what Father Time had said. He found himself ticking away quite smoothly and comfortably again, and next morning Peter was awakened by Big Ben and Little Ben both striking seven o'clock together.

Aileen E. Passmore

THE DISCONTENTED GARDEN

Once upon a time there was a king who lived in a palace in the middle of a garden. It was a magic garden, and he loved it very much, and used to walk up and down in it.

One day when he went to walk up and down in the garden, he saw that all the trees and bushes and flowers were withering away and dying. So he went up to the oak tree which stood near the gates, and said, 'Oak, Oak, what is your trouble? Why are you drooping and dying?'

And the oak said: 'O King, live for ever! I am weary of life and must die, for I am not tall like the pine tree.'

So the king went on and said to the pine tree: 'Pine Tree, Pine Tree, what is your trouble? Why are you drooping and dying?'

And the pine tree said: 'O King, live for ever! I am weary of life and must die, for I cannot bear fruit like the vine.'

So the king went on and said to the vine: 'Vine, Vine, what is your trouble? Why are you drooping and dying?'

And the vine said: 'O King, live for ever! I am weary of life and must die, for I cannot stand up straight like the peach tree.'

So the king went on and said to the peach tree: 'Peach Tree, Peach Tree, what is your trouble? Why are you drooping and dying?'

And the peach tree said: 'O King, live for ever! I am weary of life and must die, because my leaves will not stay with me all the year round, like the yew tree.'

So the king went on and said to the yew tree: 'Yew Tree, Yew Tree, what is your trouble? Why are you drooping and dying?'

And the yew tree said: 'O King, live for ever! I am weary of life and must die, for I cannot bear flowers like the hollyhock.'

So the king went on and said to the hollyhock: 'Hollyhock, Hollyhock, what is your trouble? Why are you drooping and dying?'

And the hollyhock said, 'O King, live for ever! I am weary of life and must die, because I have no scent like the wallflower.'

So the king went on and said to the wallflower: 'Wallflower, Wallflower, what is your trouble? Why are you drooping and dying?'

And the wallflower said: 'O King, live for ever! I am weary of life and must die, because I am not great like the oak.'

And the king could go no farther, for, you remember, he had already asked the oak. He was very sad, and his heart was grieved for his garden; and looking down sorrowfully, he saw at his feet a heart's-ease, a little pansy flower, smiling up at him.

'Heart's-ease, Heart's-ease,' said the king, 'how glad I am to see you looking so merry, and neither drooping nor dying.'

The heart's-ease could not talk at all grandly, but she knew she must answer the king when he was so kind as to speak to her. So she said, 'I am not very important; but I thought that if you wanted an oak, or a pine, or a vine, or a peach tree, a yew, a hollyhock or a wallflower, you would have planted one; but as I knew you wanted a heart's-ease, I thought I would be the best little heart's-ease that I can.'

Marjorie E. Procter

THE MAGIC BOOTS

An old-fashioned story

Once upon a time there was a little boy whose name was Paul. He lived with his father and mother on a farm right away in the country.

There is a lot of work to be done on a farm, and Paul's mother was always very busy. She often asked Paul to help her; and sometimes he did what she asked, but at other times he didn't want to, and would stamp his foot and say 'Bother!' when his mother called him in from his play.

One day, when the weather was nice and warm, his mother said she was going to drive into town with Paul, and buy him a pair of new boots. This was a great treat for Paul, for the town was eight miles away, and his busy mother did not often find time to go there.

When Paul returned home from the town he was a very proud boy. He carried his boots done up in a parcel, and un-wrapped them himself. They were not little boy's boots, but had fastenings like Daddy's which were much more fun than lace-holes. So he was happy that night as he lay down in his bed, under which he had carefully put his new boots.

It seemed to Paul that he had not been asleep very long when he opened his eyes and saw standing at his bedside a funny little figure. Paul was very fond of stories of gnomes, and goblins, and fairies, but he had never thought that he would really see one, yet this fat little man certainly must be a goblin. He had Paul's new boots in his hand, and was saying, 'So he does not like to help his mother, doesn't he?

That is a great pity, for she is such a loving mother, and how she works for him! Dear, dear; I must see to this at once.'

'What are you doing with my boots?' asked Paul, sitting up in bed.

'Oh, so you're awake, are you, young man?' said the goblin. 'I'll tell you what I'm going to do. This wand of mine,' and he took it from under his arm, 'is called "Love", and it can do wonders. It is going to turn your boots into magic boots.'

As he said this, he waved it three times over Paul's boots, which he still held in the other hand.

'Now,' he continued, 'they will always do just what your mother wants, and they will not care in the least for anything that you may say to them. Good-bye.'

He dropped the boots under the bed with a thump, and vanished.

Paul lay down, wondering greatly at his strange experience. Then after a time he dropped off to sleep, and knew nothing more until the morning.

After he had dressed, he took up his new boots and looked them all over, but somehow he did not want to put them on. So he slipped his feet into his old shoes and hurried down to breakfast.

'Put on your new boots, sonny,' said his mother. 'It has been raining in the night, and those old ones let in the wet.'

Paul went slowly upstairs. He sat down on his bed and put on his new boots. He wondered if anything funny would happen; but nothing did. He laced them up and marched downstairs, making quite a noise as he went.

'Run out with this skim milk to the pig, Paul,' said his mother.

Paul was just going to answer that he would go after breakfast, but he felt as if something took hold of his feet, and sent them running off to the pig-pen before he had time to say no.

'That's a good boy,' said his mother, giving him a kiss as

he came in panting. 'How quick you have been! Now carry the porridge basins in for me.'

Off trotted the boots again, taking Paul backwards and forwards from the kitchen until six basins of porridge had been carried in. It went on like that all day. As soon as his mother asked Paul to do something, off trotted the boots, and Paul had to go with them. And sometimes they even walked him off to do little helpful things without being asked! It was really fun, thought Paul, and it was so nice to hear Mother praise him for his helpfulness.

'What a kind, helpful son I have had today,' she said, giving him a good-night kiss after he was in bed.

Paul was very sleepy, but he put his arms round her neck and whispered, 'It was the magic boots, Mummy, and the goblin's magic.'

'Paul's asleep already,' said his mother, as she came downstairs, 'He's dreaming about magic and goblins. He has helped me so much today; I expect he was quite tired.'

But the old goblin, who was sitting up on the roof by the chimney, chuckled to himself, and then slid down the roof and ran home.

From A Sheaf of Stories *by Theodora Horton*
(*National Christian Education Committee*).

THE GRUMPIES

Nettie was a little girl; but she was old enough to help her mother with the dishes, and dust, and do many things that would help her when she was tired, or help her so she would not get tired; but Nettie was a shirk, and did not help if she could manage to escape.

One day her father said, 'Nettie, you are to help your mother today; she has a great deal to do, so you must take the baby in his pram and care for him this morning, and this afternoon you can play.'

'Oh dear, it is Saturday, and I want to play,' grumbled

Nettie, scowling and making a fuss, as naughty girls do sometimes.

'I am afraid you will be caught by the Grumpies, some day,' said her father. 'You shirk and leave so much for your mother to do. You leave your books on the floor, your hat on a chair, and your mother has to pick them up. I want you to be a helper to your mother, and not a grumpy little girl.'

But Nettie did not feel like helping that day. She had a book she wanted to read, so she did a very wicked thing. Right after breakfast, as soon as her father was out of the house, she began to complain that her head ached and she was sick, so sick she could not sit up. So Nettie went to her room and got in her bed. When she was sure her mother was busy, and would not come in her room, she took her book from under her pillow and began to read. She read a long time. Nettie was never sure how long, or when it happened, but all at once she felt a tug at her book, and a voice said, 'Hello, Nettie! So you are a Grumpie, like us, are you? Well, we have come to take you with us.'

Nettie looked, and all around her were the queerest-looking little creatures, with long, pointed heads, and right on the very top they had a few spears of hair, which dropped over their eyes. Before Nettie could say a word, she was carried off by these little creatures . . . and found herself, in a short time, in a most untidy room with these strange creatures all running about.

One little Grumpie, who seemed to be the spokesman, said to Nettie, 'When a new member joins the Grumpies, she has to do certain things before she can really belong, because none of us ever work when we have a new member. She has to work for a while, for that is what we are for—to make work, and never do any ourselves.'

'But I do not want to belong to the Grumpies,' said Nettie.

'Oh yes, you do,' replied the spokesman. 'You joined this morning when you left the work for your mother and went to bed. You are one of us now. . . . Now, comrades, let the fun begin!'

Nettie did not see where they came from, but these Grumpies suddenly had books in their hands, and hats, and coats, and smudgy fingers, and scissors with which they cut paper into little pieces and scattered them all about the floor; the hats they threw on the floor, too, and the coats on chairs; with their smudgy fingers they touched the white paint, and the books joined the hats and bits of paper. Their dresses were of little checked ginghams, and these they soon soiled.

'Now, Nettie, you must pick up the things, and make the room tidy, and wash our dresses, and iron them, and scrub our hands,' said the spokesman.

'I think you are a very untidy lot of creatures,' said Nettie. . . . 'You make a lot of work for me to do, and do nothing yourselves. I am not going to do a thing.'

'Spoken like a true Grumpie,' said the spokesman. 'But you will have to do this work this time, and after you have done it you are a Grumpie in reality, and will never have to work again.'

'But I told you I didn't want to look like you. You are a bad, shirking, troublesome lot, and I do not want anything to do with you.'

'Make her!' said the spokesman, and all the Grumpies rushed at Nettie like a whirlwind.

'Bang!' something sounded, and Nettie jumped. Her book was on the floor by her bed. She had fallen asleep and dropped it.

'I have been a selfish girl and a Grumpie, even if I do not look like them,' said Nettie, getting out of bed. 'I'll go right out and get the baby, and his bottle, and put him to bed, and I'll show those old Grumpies I do not want to join them after this.'

From Sandman's Bedtime Stories *by Abbie Phillips Walker (Hamish Hamilton, 1962).*

THE TEN FAIRIES

An old-fashioned story

Once upon a time, a long while ago, there was a little girl whose name was Elsa. Elsa's father and mother worked very hard and became rich. But they loved Elsa so much that they did not like her to do any work; very foolishly, they let her play all the time. So when Elsa grew up, she did not know how to do anything; she could not make bread, she could not sweep a room, she could not sew a seam; she could only laugh and sing. But she was so sweet and merry that everybody loved her. And by and by, she married one of the people who loved her and had a house of her own to take care of.

Then came hard times for Elsa! There were so many things to be done in the house, and she did not know how to do any of them! And because she had never worked at all, it made her very tired to try. Elsa's husband had a hard time of it too; he had only poor food to eat, and it was not ready at the right time, and the house looked all in a muddle. It made him sad, and that made Elsa sad, for she wanted to do everything just right.

At last, one day, Elsa's husband went away quite cross; he said to her, as he went out of the door, 'It is no wonder that the house looks so, when you sit all day with your hands in your lap.'

Little Elsa cried bitterly when he had gone, for she did not want to make her husband unhappy and cross, and she wanted the house to look nice. 'Oh dear,' she sobbed, 'I wish I could do things right! I wish I could work! I wish—I wish I had ten good fairies to work for me. Then I could keep the house.'

As she said the words, a great grey man stood before her; he was wrapped in a strange grey cloak that covered him from head to foot; and he smiled at Elsa. 'What is the matter, dear?' he said. 'Why do you cry?'

'Oh, I am crying because I do not know how to keep the house,' said Elsa. 'I cannot make bread, I cannot sweep, I cannot sew a seam. When I was a little girl I never learned to work, and now I cannot do anything right. I wish I had ten good fairies to help me.'

'You shall have them, dear,' said the grey man, and he shook his strange grey cloak. Pouf! Out popped ten tiny fairies, no bigger than that!

'These shall be your servants, Elsa,' said the grey man, 'they are faithful and clever, and they will do everything you ask them to, just right. But the neighbours might stare and ask questions if they saw these little chaps running about your house, so I will hide them away for you. Give me your hands.'

Wondering, Elsa stretched out her pretty little white hands.

'Now stretch out your little useless fingers.'

She stretched out her fingers. The grey man touched each one of the ten little fairies, and as he touched them he said their names: first the right hand—'Little Thumb; Forefinger; Thimble Finger; Ring Finger; Little Finger'—then the left hand—'Little Thumb; Forefinger; Thimble Finger; Ring Finger; Little Finger'. And as he named the fingers, one after another, the tiny fairies bowed their tiny heads; there was a fairy for every name.

'Hop! hide yourselves away!' said the grey man.

Hop! Hop! The fairies sprang to Elsa's knee, then to the palms of her hands, and then—whisk!—they were all hidden away in her fingers, a fairy in every finger. And the grey man was gone.

Elsa sat and looked with wonder at her little white hands and the ten useless fingers. But suddenly the little fingers began to stir. The tiny fairies who were hidden away there were not used to remaining still, and they were getting restless. They stirred so that Elsa jumped up and ran to the cooking table and took hold of the bread-board. No sooner had she touched the bread-board than the fairies began to work; they measured the flour, mixed the bread, kneaded the loaves and set them to rise, quicker than you could wink; and when the bread was done, it was as nice as you could wish. Then the little fairy-fingers seized the broom, and in a twinkling they were making the house clean. And so it went, all day.

There was no more crossness in that house. Elsa's husband grew so proud of her that he went about saying to everyone, 'My grandmother was a fine housekeeper, and my mother was a fine housekeeper, but neither of them could do as well as my wife. To see the work she does, you would think she had as many servants as she has fingers on her hands!'

When Elsa heard that, she used to laugh; but she never told.

From Stories to Tell to Children *by Sara Cone Bryant (Harrap, 1922). Adapted.*

THE LAZY CUCKOO

I expect you know about the cuckoo—the bird that comes in spring, and sings its own name—'Cuckoo!' This is a story about a cuckoo; but he was a wooden cuckoo, and he lived in a little wooden house. This house was really a clock; it belonged to a little girl called Janie, and her daddy had brought it back for her from Switzerland. It had a sloping roof and two shining windows, and the cuckoo was very cosy inside his little wooden house.

But the cuckoo had a job to do. Once every hour the two little doors of the house would fly open, and he had to pop out between them and cry 'Cuckoo!' At one o'clock he said it just once—'Cuckoo!' At two o'clock he said it twice— 'Cuckoo! Cuckoo!' At three o'clock he said it three times (*repeat*). And at four o'clock he said it four times (*repeat*). But when he got to twelve o'clock he had to say it *twelve* times, and that was very hard work. It used to make him dreadfully tired. How he wished he hadn't to come out at twelve o'clock!

So one day he decided that he just wouldn't do all those 'Cuckoo's' at twelve o'clock. Now it happened that that very morning Janie's mummy had said to her, 'It's such a lovely day, Janie—let's take the bus down to the sea and have a picnic on the beach and then a bathe.' For Janie's home was near the sea—not near enough to walk there, but near enough to go by bus.

'Oh, Mummy, what a lovely plan!' cried Janie, and she ran off to fetch the picnic basket, with the mugs and plates and sandwich boxes and thermos. She put them all out on the kitchen table, and her mummy made sandwiches, and hard-boiled some eggs, and packed them all in the basket with some apples and some chocolate biscuits, and put some lemonade in the thermos. Then she put in their bathing suits and towels, and they were all ready for the picnic.

Then Janie's mummy said, 'There is still a little time before the bus goes. I will go into the garden and do some weeding, and you can call out to me when the cuckoo says it's twelve o'clock. If we start out then, we shall catch the bus comfortably.'

'All right, Mummy,' said Janie. So her mummy went off down the garden, and Janie started to dress her dolly, who was called Betty, because Betty was coming on the picnic too. And she waited for her little friend the cuckoo to come out and call 'Cuckoo!' twelve times.

But, you remember, the cuckoo had decided that he wasn't going to bother to come out at twelve o'clock that day. So twelve o'clock came and went, and Janie went on dressing Betty and her mummy went on weeding in the garden. And presently she called out, 'Janie, hasn't the cuckoo said it's twelve o'clock yet?'

'No, Mummy,' said Janie.

'It seems a long time,' said her mummy; and she came indoors to look.

'Oh, Janie,' she said, 'it's ten minutes past twelve. The cuckoo didn't come out. I'm afraid we're too late for the bus.'

'Oh, Mummy, can't we have the picnic?' cried Janie, and she began to cry—she was so disappointed.

'I'm so sorry, darling,' said her mummy. 'I wish I knew where Daddy was today, because then he could take us in the car.' But Janie knew that was no good. Her daddy had a job which took him all over the place in his car, and they never knew where he would be. So she just went on crying.

'Never mind,' said her mummy. 'We can have our picnic in the garden instead.'

'It's not the same,' sobbed Janie. She went and stood under the cuckoo clock, and called up to the bird inside it, 'You naughty cuckoo! Why didn't you come out? You've spoiled our lovely picnic, you bad bird!'

The cuckoo heard what Janie said, and he felt very sorry. He had never thought that his laziness would spoil Janie's happy day. He tried to call out to her, 'Oh, Janie, I am sorry. I'm really, *really* sorry.'

Of course Janie couldn't hear him. But sometimes if you have done something wrong, and you are really, *really* sorry, things do come right in the end, after all. And that's how it was with Janie, as you shall hear.

Janie's mummy had fetched the table-cloth. 'Here you are, Janie,' she said. 'Go and put it on the table in the garden, and I'll bring the picnic out.' So Janie went out, very slowly, because she was still so disappointed. She started to put the cloth on the table. And just at that very moment what should drive up to the gate but her daddy's motor-car, and there was her daddy himself jumping out.

'Oh, hullo, Daddy,' Janie cried. She was *so* pleased to see him!

'Hullo, my Janie,' he said, as he picked her up in his arms. 'Why, you've been crying! Whatever is the matter?'

So Janie told him the whole sad story about the naughty

cuckoo. And then what do you think her daddy said? 'I'll tell you what we'll do. We'll put you and Mummy and the picnic in the car, and I'll drive you down to the sea—I have to go that way—and I'll have a picnic with you too on the beach. What about that?'

'Oh, hurray, hurray!' shouted Janie, and she ran in to tell her mummy.

'That *will* be nice!' said her mummy. 'What a good thing I boiled three eggs. Now we can have our picnic after all, and with Daddy too.'

So off they went—Mummy and Daddy and Janie and the picnic and Betty—I hope you haven't forgotten Betty. And when the cuckoo heard them drive away, he said, 'I'm so glad it was all right in the end for Janie. And I'll never be a lazy cuckoo again.' And he never was.

THE GRUMBLER

Once upon a time there was a boy who used to grumble. He was at it all the time. When it was time to go to bed he grumbled because he was not tired, and when his grandfather called him in the morning, he grumbled because he was. He grumbled over his slice of cake because it was not enough, and over his school work because it was too much. Once he ran in a race at a picnic, and sulked and grumbled because he did not win. Next time he won, and made himself and everybody else unhappy because he did not like his prize.

No one liked this boy, because selfish, grumbling boys are not nice to meet, and if there are such things as selfish, grumbling girls, I suppose people would not like them very much either.

One night this boy was sent to bed a bit earlier than usual, for grumbling. By and by, with a dark frown on his face, he fell asleep, and, of course, he dreamed. He thought he was sitting on a hillside in the sunshine all alone. And he was still grumbling. From time to time he kicked the stump of an old tree lying near his foot, and at last he decided to go home. Just at that moment, however, there was a slight rustling sound, and out of a gorse bush there stepped a fairy with a tiny silver wand in her hand.

'Good morning,' she said. 'I hope I find you happy.'

'No,' said Walter—that was his name, 'you don't find me happy; I never am happy.'

'Dear me,' said the fairy with a little smile, 'dear me.' Then, after looking at him for a long time, she remarked, 'Seeing you are not a great success as a boy, is there anything else you would rather be?'

'It's no use wanting to be anything else,' said Walter.

'Oh yes, it is,' said the fairy.

> 'For I have magic, art and power
> To change to bird, or beast, or flower.'

Walter thought for a moment. It cannot be worse, he thought; and it will probably be a great deal better. Then he said, 'Make me a bird.'

The fairy stepped forward and touched him with her wand, and the next moment he felt himself rising from the ground. It felt fearfully strange, and when he stretched out his hands to save himself from falling, he discovered they were wings. By and by he began to feel less strange and timid. Looking down, he saw that he had already risen high above the trees. Up and up he flew, feeling almost as if he could reach the sun.

'This is the life,' he thought. 'No more horrid sums to do, no baby to mind, no errands to run.' So free and happy did he feel that he opened his beak and began to sing. At that moment a shadow fell, and looking up he saw another bird hovering between him and the sun. One glance was enough, for Walter had often seen a hawk, and he knew what was likely to be his fate. His heart began to thump, and his brain turned sick with fear. Fast as he flew to earth, the shadow flew faster, until, just as the hawk whirled above him and prepared to strike, the frightened bird found a tiny hole in the trunk of a tree, and was safe.

'This will never do,' said Walter, as he began to recover from his fright. 'I can never go on like this. I wonder if that fairy is about.'

Cautiously putting his head out of his hiding-place, he saw the fairy just beneath him on the grass. Feeling safe when she was near, he popped out of the hollow trunk, and fell at her feet.

'Fairy,' he said, 'I don't want to be a bird any more; what else have you got?'

'Why,' she answered, 'did I not tell you

> That I have magic, art and power
> To change to bird, or beast, or flower'?

'Is a rabbit a beast?' asked Walter. The fairy said it might count as one. 'Well, then, make me a rabbit,' said Walter.

The instant the silver wand touched him, his wish was granted. There he sat in his lovely soft fur coat, as real as could be. Feeling hungry, he began to nibble a little blade of grass.

What sound was that? The rabbit turned an anxious eye towards a clump of bushes. He soon knew what it was. There was no mistaking that great shaggy head with its lolling tongue and gleaming teeth. How Walter ran! Ears back, eyes bulging, paws madly leaping through the air! Fast as he sped, he was not fast enough, and just as he sprang into a bush which hid a burrow, the dog snapped at him and got a mouthful of his fur.

All night long he lay trembling in that narrow den, but just as it was turning light he heard the sound of silver footsteps, and ventured out to meet the fairy. She smiled when she saw him, and when he said, 'I don't like being a beast; I want you to turn me into a flower,' she smiled again. However, she briskly tapped him with her wand, and he became a rose, a red rose, tall and handsome, growing in a garden.

He looked about him nervously, but everything was so still and lovely that Walter thought, 'I've found a spot where I can be happy and at peace at last.' Tired out with all he had passed through, he closed his petals and fell fast asleep. He was wakened by feeling rather tickled, and looking down, he saw that a green caterpillar was crawling up his stem. Walter shook himself, but the caterpillar held on. Half a minute later it arrived at a leaf, and calmly began its breakfast.

'Here,' cried Walter, 'get off! Do you know what you are doing? You are eating ME!'

A little later, as the fairy passed through the garden, she heard a sound of crying, and found the face of the rose all wet with tears. 'Change me back, again, Fairy, oh change me back again, please. I never knew how well off I was when I was a boy.'

The fairy stretched out her wand, but before it touched him he heard a loud voice: 'Walter! TIME TO GET UP.'

'All right, Mother,' called Walter. 'Thank you.'

'Well,' said his mother to herself, 'that is the first time I ever knew that boy say "Thank you" when I told him to get up.'

You see, Walter really had given up grumbling.

From The Skylark's Bargain *by G. H. Charnley*
(Allenson & Co., Ltd.), Abridged and adapted.

LOOK-AT-ME, THE PIGLET

Once there was a mother pig who had twelve little piglets. There were so many piglets that their mother couldn't think of names for all of them. But one of the piglets had a name. Everyone called him 'Look-at-me'.

Can you guess why he had that name? It was because he was always saying, 'Look at me! Aren't I clever?' When all the piglets were running about in the sty, he would say, 'Look at me. Aren't I clever? I can curl my tail up tighter than any of you.' And when the farmer let them all go out in the field to look for tasty titbits, he would call out, 'Look at me. Aren't I clever? I'm finding more titbits than any of you.'

One day, when Mother Pig and her piglets were out in the field, Look-at-me thought he would go and see what was on the other side of the field. So off he ran. 'Look at me!' he called as he ran. 'I'm braver than any of you—I'm going off all on my own.' He ran and he ran, and all the time he kept calling, 'Look at me. Aren't I brave?'

Presently he came to the edge of the field, where there was a hedge. And in the hedge there was a hole. So the little piglet crawled through it. 'Look at me,' he called. 'Aren't I clever? I got through that hole.' But of course nobody heard him; his mother and brothers and sisters were much too far away, right across the field.

On the other side of the hedge there was a road, and Look-at-me started to trot along it. 'Look at me!' he kept calling. But after a while he stopped calling; he found that he didn't know where he was, or where he was going. So he turned round, and ran back. 'I'll find that hole,' he thought, 'and crawl through it again.' But he couldn't find it. He ran up and down the hedge looking everywhere, but he couldn't find the way through. He began to cry,—'Week! Week! Week!'—that is the way piglets cry.

Just then he heard the most dreadful noise. It was the farmer coming along on his tractor. But of course Look-at-me didn't know that, and it frightened him dreadfully. He just ran away as fast as he could, crying, 'Week! Week! Week!'

'Why, there's one of the piglets!' said the farmer. 'He must have got out somehow.' And he jumped off the tractor and ran after Look-at-me till he caught him. Then he picked him up, and opened the gate into the field, and carried him through it, and took him back to his mother and his brothers and sisters. And wasn't Look-at-me glad to be back with them again!

And do you know, after that he stopped saying, 'Look at me!', and his brothers and sisters liked him much better when he wasn't so conceited.

MARMALADE KITTEN AND WHITE KITTEN

Once there were two cats. One was marmalade and the other was white. And each cat had a kitten. The marmalade cat had a marmalade kitten, and the white cat had a white kitten. They were quite different. And the two mother cats brought up their children quite differently too.

Mother Marmalade Cat was very strict with her kitten. He had to get up the minute she called him, and go to bed the minute she told him, and eat whatever she gave him to eat. He hardly ever had cream—only as a very special treat. And what a lot of washing he got! Mother White Cat was not strict with her kitten at all. He could go to bed just when he liked and get up just when he felt like it. He ate whatever he fancied, and had cream so often that he grew quite tired of it. His mother only washed him when he wanted to be washed, and he didn't want to be washed often; so he got very dirty.

But although those two kittens were brought up so differently, they were alike in one thing. They were both *miserable*! Marmalade Kitten wished he could do what he liked when he liked, and eat what he liked, and have more fun. And White Kitten got pains in his tummy because he ate too much cream, and his lovely white fur was all dirty and draggled because he didn't like it being washed, and that made him very uncomfortable.

So one day the two mother cats got together and had a chat about their children. 'Whatever can we do about them?' said Mother Marmalade Cat. 'It is dreadful to see them so miserable.'

'I know,' said Mother White Cat. 'We'll swap them. You take mine, and I'll take yours, and we'll see what a change will do.'

And that's what they did. White Kitten went to live with Mother Marmalade Cat, and Marmalade Kitten went to live with Mother White Cat.

White Kitten was very surprised when, quite early in the evening, Mother Marmalade Cat said, 'Now, kitten, bedtime!' But he was really very tired, and glad to go to bed. And he had such a lovely long sleep that in the morning, when Mother Marmalade Cat called, 'Time to get up!', up he jumped quite spry and perky. Then Mother Marmalade Cat gave him a good wash, whether he wanted it or not. 'Your fur is disgracefully dirty,' she said; and she worked so hard that she made it shining white, and White Kitten really liked it better that way. It was more comfortable and didn't tickle so much. Then there was breakfast; and White Kitten was so tired of cream that he was really quite glad there wasn't any.

Meantime, Marmalade Kitten was enjoying himself very much with Mother White Cat. He was allowed to stay up later than he had ever done before and get up when he liked in the morning, and that was a lovely change. And he was having all the cream he wanted. But he didn't much like not being washed, and so he learnt to wash himself.

After a time the two mother cats brought the two kittens to be swapped back again. And two very happy little kittens went back to their mothers. They had had a wonderful time; but they were very glad to be home again.

From a story by Dorothy Allen

A HOLE IN YOUR STOCKING

Once there was a beetle who loved another beetle. Oh dear me! How he did love her! So he went to her house to ask her to marry him. He knocked on the door. Bang! Bang! 'May I come in?'

'Oh dear me, no! I am busy resting this fine afternoon.' He looked up, and, sure enough, the window curtains were tightly drawn.

'But listen to me,' he said. 'I have come to ask you to marry me. Open the door so that I can do it properly.'

'Why ever should I marry you?' she asked. But she drew the curtains aside a little to take a good look at him.

'Why should you marry me?' he said. 'Well, there are reasons enough. I am quite the most handsome beetle in all the parish. My fine black armour is smooth and shiny. I hold my pincers bravely, my legs are elegant and my eyes are bright. You will never meet a beetle more beautiful than I.'

'Listen to him!' she said. 'Just listen to him! All he can think of is his own beauty. If he thinks himself so fine, he won't think the more of me.' And she shouted through the door, 'Go away, now, do. I am beginning to feel sleepy.'

But still he knocked, and still he cried, 'Open the door, do open the door. Only open it a little. You will see for yourself—so handsome, so strong. There's not a beetle as strong as me in all the parish. My legs are firm, my pincers are cruel. Woe betide the enemy who is taken in my jaws! There's not a beetle alive dare face me in mortal combat. How happy you should be to have such a husband!'

'That's all very well,' she said, 'but what about me? You have only to lose your temper with me, and then what price your strength? I'd be lucky to keep my head on my shoulders. Take your strength away. I can do well enough without it in my home.'

'Oh, but listen to me! Do listen to me! That is not all.

Really it isn't. I'm the richest beetle hereabouts. . . .' And he began to tell her all he had. 'I have three pretty boxes all full of threepenny bits. I have seven new packets of glass-headed pins, all different colours, not one the same. A peacock's feather, and a piece of red seaweed, a drawerful of postage stamps and new paint in tubes. As for the larder—I have seven shelves of sweeties in big glass jars, a shelf of honeycombs, and another of jellies and pink blancmange. If you had one for dinner every day of the year, you would not reach the end of them.'

'Oh stop it, do,' she said. 'How tired I am! If you have so much already, you cannot want me. Go away, now, do, and let me go to sleep.' And she slammed the window to, so that she could not hear him any more.

And then how sad he was! He began to cry. He turned round about and was going down the road, the big tears splashing in the dust. She was looking after him, as he went down the road, for after all she was curious to see what he looked like. And she saw two big holes in his stockings, one in either heel. She saw them clearly as he went down the road. She opened the window and called out after him, 'Hey! You there! You so rich and strong and beautiful! Here you come courting with holes in your stockings. Who looks after you at home to allow such a thing?'

'There's no one to look after me,' he said. 'My granny is so blind she sits by the fire all day. My mother takes in washing, and she has no time for me. And as for my sister, she is down at the end of the garden playing cards and talking to the neighbours. No one bothers about me, and so I get holes in my stockings.'

'Come along back here,' she cried. 'I can't have you going away from my house looking like that.' And she had him in, took up her needle and thread and darned up his stockings and sewed on a button, and, oh well—there you are! By the time she had done with him she loved him so dearly that when he asked her to marry him, she didn't say no.

So when you go out courting, you take it from me—go with a full heart and a hole in your stocking, and then you, too, shall marry a wife.

From The Tooter *by Dina Ross (Faber and Faber, 1951).*
Slightly adapted.

FISH FOR TEA

One day Rory McWhirter's father said to him, 'I have a holiday today, Rory. Would you like to come fishing with me?'

'Oh yes, Daddy,' said Rory. 'That would be fun.'

So first of all they went into the garden and dug up a fine supply of worms. Then they went to Mrs. Busy's shop. That was the name Rory had given to the lady who ran the shop, because she was round and jolly and bustled about just like a busy bee. She sold everything, from comics to cornflakes. First of all they bought some bottles of lemonade, and then Rory spent fourpence of his pocket money on lollipops.

'I'm going fishing with my daddy,' he told Mrs. Busy.

'Well, good luck to you,' said Mrs. Busy, as she handed him the lollipops.

Rory walked along beside his daddy, feeling very important. When they came near the river, they passed a cottage where three boys were in the garden. They called to Rory over the fence, 'Hullo, Rory! Going fishing? Can we come with you? We've all got rods.' But Rory didn't want them, and he pretended not to see them. He just walked on, and then they began calling after him, 'Silly old Rory! Silly old Rory!'

'Who are those rude boys?' asked his daddy.

'They're Tom, Dick and Harry,' said Rory. 'We don't want them, do we?'

When Rory and his daddy came to the river, they settled down to fish in the warm sunshine. But every time they nearly had a bite, there was a 'plop!' and a stone landed in the water and scared the fish away. It was those boys from the cottage—they were paying Rory back for not letting them come fishing with him.

Then Mr. McWhirter grew drowsy, and tried to drop off to sleep, and so did Rory; but every time they were nearly asleep, a most annoying fly came buzzing round their noses. But it wasn't really a fly; it was those naughty boys again. They had climbed up into a tree over the river, and were letting down a tuft of grass tied on the end of a string. It made an excellent fly. At last Mr. McWhirter saw what was happening, and caught hold of the string.

'Little wretches!' he snorted.

'Spoiling our day!' said Rory crossly.

Just then they saw Mrs. McWhirter coming along in a great hurry. 'I've just had a telegram from Scotland,' she cried. 'Your Auntie Alice is coming today for tea, Rory. So you must catch lots of fish for us all to eat at tea-time.'

Rory was very pleased—his auntie was great fun. 'Good old Auntie Alice!' he said, and danced for joy.

'Now we've got to catch fish, young man,' said his daddy, 'and what's more, *lots* of fish. How are we going to do it?'

They thought for a moment, and then Daddy said, 'We'll ask those young scamps from the cottage to come and help us.' So Rory went racing off to find Tom, Dick and Harry. 'My daddy says, will you help us catch fish?' he called. So, out the three boys came with their rods, and so there were five fishermen sitting side by side in silence on the river bank, waiting for a bite.

But they had no luck. They had fine rods, the best and juiciest worms, and perfect quietness; but not a single fish was in the basket.

'Oh, well, I expect we'd better stop and have a drink,' said Mr. McWhirter.

'Good idea!' cried Rory and Tom, Dick and Harry. They all started to drink lemonade. But just as he was putting the bottle to his mouth, Tom cried, 'Hi! My float bobbed down.' He whisked it up, and on the end was a fat little fish. And after that they all began to catch fish.

'That will make a lovely tea for Auntie Alice,' said Rory, as he popped all the fish into the basket. 'Thanks for coming to help, Tom, Dick and Harry.'

They carried the basket back in triumph, and Mrs. McWhirter was delighted. So was Auntie Alice when she arrived. The three boys stayed to tea; and when Auntie Alice heard about how they had caught the fish all together, she was very grateful to Rory and his daddy and his three friends.

THE TEST

A story of two boys in space

This is a story about the future—the time when space travel is so easy that anyone can visit the moon and the planets.

Rodney and Gavin Brown were twins, though Rodney was a little bit the older; and so of course they had their birthday on the same day. And on that day their grandfather said, 'Now, you two, I've got a special treat for you as a birthday present. You've heard about the new planet that has been discovered—so new that it hasn't even got a name yet. They've started running space trips to it, and I've booked seats for you both on one of them.'

'Whoopee! Smashing!' shouted the twins. 'Thank you, Grandpa.' They could hardly believe their good luck when the great day came and the family came with them to the space-port to see them off, in the spaceship *Meteor*. They had been told to have baths and put on clean clothes for the trip, and now they were waiting to go aboard the ship. They could see it at the top of the huge rocket which was to launch it.

'I've got something here for you to take on the trip, boys,' said their father. 'I'm going to lend you my precious field-glasses. Rodney, you take charge of them, because you're the elder; but mind you and Gavin share them fairly between you, and take great care of them.'

Just then a voice called out, 'All passengers for the *Meteor* into the testing-room, please.' They all went into a waiting-room, and after waiting their turn, the boys were taken into a small room where there was a panel on the wall with four holes in it.

'Now,' said a man in a white coat, 'everyone who goes to the New Planet has to be clean, inside as well as outside. We can't have anything bad taken up there. So just stand over here one at a time.' He put Rodney before the panel, and pressed a button, and lights came on in all the four holes.

'Nice and clear,' said the man. 'Now you.' So Gavin had his turn, and he was all right too. So they said good-bye to the family, and got into the lift, which whizzed them up to the top of the tall tower which held the rocket. They could see the family waving below. They were shut in, and then came the great roar of the blast-off, and they were shot out into space. They soon got used to seeing nothing outside the windows but empty space with a few stars here and there. After a time they went to sleep, and when they woke up they could look back and see the earth far away behind them, looking like a moon.

Presently they saw in front of them what looked like another small moon. 'That is the New Planet,' said the space hostess, as she brought them a meal. They sat watching the planet get bigger and bigger, till at last, when it was huge, the sound of the motors changed, and they knew they were going down. Then *Meteor* put out three great legs, and— thud! they had landed on the New Planet.

'We spend half an hour on the planet,' said the pilot, 'and then we go back to earth. But first you will all be taking the test again.'

So again the boys waited their turn. They watched the passengers go one by one into a building, and then come out dressed in strange metal suits with clear-glass helmets. It took a long time, but there was plenty to look at—queer spiky hills and strange coloured rocks.

'Oh,' said Rodney suddenly, looking through the field-glasses, 'I thought I saw a little man with green horns peeping over that rock.'

'Let me see,' said Gavin.

'No,' said Rodney. 'I want to see if he pops up again.'

'But it's my turn,' insisted Gavin. 'You're a selfish beast, Rodney.' He made a grab at the glasses, and the two boys started to fight. They were interrupted by the space hostess, who said, 'Now, boys—your turn next to be tested.'

Again they found themselves in the little room with the panel and the four holes. This time Gavin went first. The operator pressed the button, and up came the lights; but— the second one from the left was green.

'H'm! Jealousy!' said the man. 'I'm afraid we couldn't let you out on the planet with that on you. Sorry, old chap— you'll have to go back to the ship and wait.' Then he tested Rodney. The button was pressed, and there were the lights again; but this time the third one was red!

'Some selfishness there—and anger too,' said the operator. 'I'm afraid you'll have to wait with your brother.'

So in the spaceship they had to stay till the other passengers came back and they set off home again. It was very hard to have to tell the family that they hadn't been allowed to land on the New Planet—and why. But Grandpa says he will give them another trip for their birthday next year; and Rodney and Gavin are practising hard to be fit for it.

THE THREE WISHES

A modern version of an old story

Ian and Linda were two children who lived with their parents on the edge of a little town. The father grew vegetables and took them in to market with a horse and cart; the mother made money by sewing.

But sad days came for this little family. The parents both died, and Ian and Linda were left alone. Fortunately they were old enough by this time to look after themselves; Ian had learnt from his father how to keep the vegetable garden going, and Linda could sew like her mother. So for a time they got on pretty well.

But after a while the old horse Prince began to grow too feeble for his work, and the old cart became rickety, while Linda said that the sewing machine was old too, and would not last much longer. And they had not enough money to buy a new horse or sewing machine.

One day, when they were in town together, they were walking along discussing this sad state of things, when Linda suddenly exclaimed, 'Oh, Ian, do look at that funny little man. What queer clothes he has.'

'Yes,' said Ian, 'and he looks as if he doesn't know his way about. Oh, he is going to cross the road, and he hasn't learnt his curb drill—he isn't looking left and right——' and Ian dashed forward as he spoke, and pulled the little man back just as a huge lorry thundered past.

'Oh dear me!' exclaimed the little gentleman. 'That was a very narrow squeak! We don't have great monsters like that where I come from.'

'And where do you come from?' inquired Ian curiously. He really was a very odd little man.

'Oh, up there somewhere,' said the little man, pointing to the sky. 'On one of those things you call planets. Oh dear, I really do feel very giddy.'

'You must come home with us,' said Linda, 'and rest a bit.' So they took him back to their house, and tucked him up on a couch to rest, and gave him a drink of water and whatever he fancied to eat—he seemed to like best the raw oats which Linda used to make porridge. 'It's more like what we have at home,' he told them.

At last he seemed to feel much better, and said he must be going.

'Oh, do stay for the night,' they begged.

'No, thank you,' he said. 'It's very kind of you, but I must be getting back. But I am very grateful to you kind young people, and I should like to reward you for all your trouble. I have the power to grant wishes, and I shall give you three—one wish each, and the third one between you. You must both guess it, and the first two wishes will not come true until you have guessed the third. Good-bye and good luck!' And suddenly he was gone.

'Isn't it exciting?' said Linda. 'What shall you wish for, Ian?'

'I know exactly what I want,' said Ian, 'a little red van to drive the vegetables to market. What shall you wish for, Linda?'

'A sewing machine, of course,' said his sister. 'A blue one like I saw in a shop, that will sew ever so quickly and ever so quietly. Oh, come on, Ian—let's wish now.'

So they screwed up their faces and wished for a red van and a blue sewing machine. But the old machine still stood on the table, and old Prince still stood hanging his head in the stall.

'Well, that wasn't much good,' said Ian.

'Oh, but we've forgotten the third wish,' cried Linda. 'We have to wish that together—whatever can it be?' They thought and thought, and wished and wished, and then they began to argue, and grew so tired and cross that after a miserable day they were quite worn out by bedtime, and fell asleep at once.

Linda woke up in the night, and heard Ian in his room tossing and muttering in his sleep. 'Poor Ian!' she thought. 'He does need that van so badly. I do wish he could have it.' And then she fell asleep.

Presently Ian woke up, and heard Linda in her room breathing very quietly and peacefully. 'Dear Linda!' he thought. 'How much she would love that sewing machine! How I wish she could have it!' And then he, too, fell asleep.

In the morning Linda got up first and went downstairs to take in the milk. But she came running upstairs again, calling, 'Ian, Ian, come and see!' She was so excited that she could hardly speak. Ian ran down, and there at the door stood the very same little red van he had been longing for.

'Oh,' cried Linda, 'do you think perhaps my sewing machine may have come too?' She peeped into the sitting-room, hardly daring to breathe, and there on the table stood the very same little blue sewing machine she had been longing for.

'But how has it happened?' cried Ian. 'What have we wished?'

'Well,' said Linda, 'I wished in the night that you should have your van.'

'And I wished for you to have your sewing machine,' said Ian. 'That must be it.'

'But that makes two wishes,' said Linda.

'No, it doesn't,' said Ian. 'It was the same wish really. Each of us had to wish for the other's wish to come true before we got our own.'

'Dear little sky man,' said Linda. 'How kind he was! I wish we could thank him.'

'Well, I'm going to try driving my van,' said Ian.

'And I'll try using my sewing machine,' said Linda. 'Oh, isn't it fun?'

THE BOSSY BULLDOZER

Once upon a time there was a young bulldozer. He was very smart, with red and green paint, and he worked with a whole family of cranes and concrete mixers and pile-drivers and trucks to build a new sea wall. It should have been a lovely job in the long summer days, with the sea so close; but the trouble was the bulldozer. True, he was very clever and he worked very hard, but he was so bossy, and there were such a lot of squabbles.

High up on one of the tall wooden piles that had been driven into the shingle sat a friendly crab called Clara. Now Clara often got worried, and so did the seagulls flying overhead, when they saw how many times the work on the sea wall stopped to settle an argument. They knew what would happen if the job wasn't finished before the big gales of wind came in the winter. The sea would come sweeping in and flood people's homes with water. So the seagulls flew low, calling 'Hurry up!' and 'Get on with it!'; but no one paid any attention to them. And Clara, as she sat on her wooden post, just longed to help; but she couldn't shovel sand or drive piles, so what could she do?

One afternoon the bulldozer was having a chat with his friend the concrete mixer.

'Lucky, aren't we?' sighed the concrete mixer, as he gently rolled his dinner round and round inside him to mix it up. 'Here we are by the sea, with the sun shining and lots of children watching us.'

'Yes,' replied the bulldozer, 'and did you hear what they said about ME this morning?' And he preened himself to show off his smart green paint. 'They said . . .'

'Oh, I know,' broke in the concrete mixer. 'They said what a *wonderful* bulldozer you were! I've heard it all before.'

'Well, it's true, isn't it?' cried the bulldozer, up in arms. 'I do all the work in this place. Just where would you all be without me, I'd like to know? All you others are just stuck in the mud.' And he whizzed and turned round, and then pushed a perfectly enormous pile of sand and pebbles into the sea. 'And that's more than *you* can do!' he called up to the tall cranes above him. But the cranes didn't say anything, so the bulldozer went on. 'You're just a lot of swanks up there!' he jeered.

There was absolute silence after this very rude remark. Then one of the tallest cranes quietly bent his hook down and firmly caught the bossy bulldozer by the seat of his pants, swung him across the beach and plunged him right down into the deep water.

'Rotten beastly cheats, you cranes!' stormed the bull-dozer, as he landed on a rock at the bottom of the sea. 'I'll pay you back for this!'

It was very wet and uncomfortable down there, and he went on fussing and raging so that foam and bubbles came up to the top of the water. The kind-hearted concrete mixer saw them, and longed to come to the rescue. But of course he couldn't.

Gradually the bulldozer stopped being angry and started to be sorry for himself. In fact, he started to cry, and great big tears rolled down the green and red paint and made him wetter than ever.

'Everyone's beastly!' he sobbed. 'Why are they all so horrid to me? I hate them all.'

Just then Clara slid down her wooden post into the sea and began to talk to him.

'The concrete mixer sent me down to see how you were getting on,' she began. But the bulldozer only grunted.

'You must be feeling very wet,' Clara went on in a kindly voice.

'It's terrible!' groaned the bulldozer. 'Those awful swanky cranes . . .'

'It's a funny thing, you know,' began Clara, feeling a little trembly because the bulldozer was so big and she was so small. 'But they do say that if you point a finger at another person, you point three at yourself at the same time.'

'What?' snapped the bulldozer. 'Don't believe it!'

But a moment or two later he couldn't help trying it. He pointed his finger at Clara, and—why—yes! There were three other fingers curled back and pointing at him! It was true.

'Humph!' he grunted, and then he was quiet for a bit.

'That means,' Clara went on, 'that if you think someone else is wrong, and point your finger at him, it means that you're three times as much wrong, because three fingers are pointing at you.'

'Oh,' said the bulldozer. And he thought about it. Was it really the cranes who were swanky? Could it possibly be him? And did what Clara said mean that he was three times as swanky as the cranes?

'There's just one other thing, before I go up again,' said Clara, 'and that is that the crane's hook and chain are still hooked on to you. If you felt like sending up a message—you could be up in two ticks.'

The bulldozer splashed around a bit and rubbed his nose. At last he said to Clara, 'Ask the crane to pull me up.'

So presently there was a terrific squelch and a splutter and a great fountain of water, and up came the bulldozer from the sea bottom.

The concrete mixer rattled and jostled her stones around inside her to show how glad she was to see him again. The bulldozer shook himself, and water came shooting off him like a waterfall. He coughed the sand and seaweed out of his throat, and then he said 'Sorry' to the cranes for being such a nuisance and so rude. It was the most difficult thing he had ever done in his life.

The sun shone on his paint, which was as lovely as ever; and then they all set to work again. The bulldozer shovelled and pushed, and the cranes lifted the piles and put them into position, and the pile-drivers went, 'Bang! Bang! Bang!' All the children were thrilled to see everything working again. The seagulls flying overhead were specially glad; they called out, 'Well done! Well done!'

And Clara the crab sat on the top of her wooden pile and thought to herself, 'I'm not very big, and I can't shovel sand or mix concrete; but I do think I was useful today.'

And that is the end of the story.

Rosalie Procter

THE POLE AND THE PYLONS

There was once a fir tree which had one great longing—he wanted to be a Christmas tree. Every December many of his friends in the plantation on the sheltered side of the downs were taken off to be sold in the big towns, and the tales of their adventures were whispered among the branches of the fir trees which were left.

'The children fasten shining coloured balls on you,' said one, 'and candles too!'

'And you stand in a place of honour near the fire,' said another, 'and are hung with presents and silver tinsel. And everyone who comes into the room says "How lovely!" '

The fir tree would sigh with joy at the very thought of how warm and gay it would be. He would look out over the downs and pity the giant pylons which carried the electricity and the tall telegraph poles which carried the news, and think how cold they must be out there.

But the years went by and the fir tree grew taller and taller till he was far too big to be a Christmas tree. The only other thing that he knew he could be was a telegraph pole; but he dreaded the thought of that. He just couldn't bear to think of being stripped of all his branches and made to stand alone in the wind and the rain, with no other friendly trees near him. But he went on growing tall and strong, and, sure enough, the day came when he was cut down to be made into a telegraph pole.

Just as he was being taken off, the old oak at the corner of the plantation, who was his great friend, called out, 'Cheer up! It may be the best thing for you. You know what happens to Christmas trees in the end, don't you?'

'No,' said the fir tree.

'Well, they get a bit too warm. They're cut up into logs, and put on the fire, and go up the chimney in flames. But you'll have a long life as a telegraph pole—and I think it will be interesting.'

'Humph!' muttered the fir tree. He did feel a little better, though he didn't quite know what the oak tree meant. However, when finally he was set up, and all his wires fixed, not far from his old home in the plantation, he began to understand. He carried the wires to the farm in the hollow, and all sorts of interesting news ran through his head. Sometimes it would be the farmer ringing the garage because the tractor had broken down; another evening he would hear the farmer's little daughter Gillian having a chat with her Granny miles and miles away in London. Once it was the farmer's wife calling the doctor because Gillian was ill. And another day he had a great thrill—he heard Gillian telling her Granny that she had a new baby brother.

So the fir tree felt very important and happy. True, it was cold and bleak in the winter time, but there were lovely summer days too, when he could look down into the valley and watch the hay-making and all the work on the farm. The seagulls brought him news from the old oak tree and his other friends who were still in the plantation.

Then he tried to make friends with the pylons; but the trouble was that they were very important, carrying all the electricity for the whole district—and they knew it. So they kept their tall heads in the air and looked down their noses at the fir tree.

'Only a telegraph pole!' he seemed to hear them whispering down their wires. So the fir tree felt very lonely sometimes, and missed his friends. He longed above all for the pylons to notice him and be nice to him.

One moonlight night, just after all the hay had been harvested into two big ricks, the fir tree heard the pylons whispering and laughing together.

'Why don't we have a dance?' suggested one.

'Why not?' echoed another. 'No one needs electricity just now. Fancy ironing a pair of trousers or milking a cow or having a permanent wave in the middle of the night! Ha! Ha! Ha!' And the pylons laughed their heads off. The fir tree couldn't think of any answer to what they were saying, though he knew somehow that it was wrong. He did say, 'What about sick people? They need a light. . . .' But his voice was carried away as the pylons began to dance. The wind blew the wires wildly round them in the moonlight as they swayed and sang. Nearer and nearer they came to the fir tree.

'Come on and join us!' they called to him. 'It's fun!'

'No, no,' shouted back the fir tree.

'Be a sport! We're all doing it.'

The fir tree felt terrible. He couldn't bear to say no, the very first time the pylons were friendly; and yet—and yet——

'You're afraid!' scoffed the pylons.

'No, I'm not!' blazed back the fir tree. Then, forgetting everything, he joined in the dance.

All went well till one of the pylons tripped and fell across his wires. 'Snap! Snap! Snap!'—and they were broken. Just at that very moment there was a small blaze of light over near the farm.

'It's a fire near the hay-ricks!' cried the fir tree. 'And we cannot call for the fire engine,' he groaned. The pylons slipped back to their places, very subdued, and watched helplessly as the flames rose higher and higher. Soon they knew that a rick was alight.

'Oh dear, oh dear!' sobbed the fir tree. 'All that hard work wasted, and that lovely hay going up in smoke!' Then suddenly coming along the road they saw a little light. The moon was so bright that they could see what it was—Gillian on her bicycle in her pyjamas, going to fetch the fire engine. Not long after, the siren sounded, and 'Clang, clang, clang' went the fire bells, as three or four engines came dashing to the farm. Very soon the fire was out, just in time to save the second rick.

After that wild summer's night, the pylons were very different. They were really sad for the farmer losing the precious hay, and told the fir tree that it was all their fault.

'No, it wasn't,' said the fir tree. 'It was *my* fault. I knew something might happen on the farm—it often does in the night if a cow gets ill.' They argued away till the morning, when men came to mend the broken wires. Then they all felt better.

In fact, they became great friends. The fir tree told the pylons the news that came along the wires, and they often laughed together. The pylons told the fir tree about the homes and shops and hospitals they supplied with heat and light, and the factories they fed with power to make cars and aeroplanes and vacuum cleaners.

One day the fir tree called a seagull and sent a message to his friend the old oak tree at the corner of the plantation. 'Tell him,' said the fir tree, 'that he was quite right—it is good to be a telegraph pole. And give him my love.'

Rosalie Procter

THE WISE OLD DWARF

There once was a little elf called Dora. She was pretty and rich, and her parents spoiled her terribly. She was always laughing. She laughed from early morning until late at night; she was happy about everything, and never gave sadness or sorrow a thought.

In the same forest where Dora made her home there lived a dwarf by the name of Peldron. He was in everything the exact opposite of Dora. While Dora was for ever smiling at all the beauty and goodness about her, Peldron worried because there was so much misery in the world, and especially in the world of elves and dwarfs.

One day Dora had to do an errand at the shoemaker's in Elves' Village. And what do you think happened? She met that boring and long-faced Peldron. Dora was sweet, but, because everyone liked her, she was a bit conceited too.

Boldly she ran towards Peldron, grabbed his pretty dwarf's hat and, from a distance, laughed with the hat in her hand.

Peldron was really cross; he stamped on the ground and called, 'Give me back my hat, give it back immediately.'

But Dora did no such thing, ran farther away and finally hid the hat in a hollow tree. Then she quickly continued on her way to the shoemaker's.

After looking for it a long time, Peldron did find his hat. He couldn't take a joke, and especially not from Dora, whom he didn't like at all. Listlessly he went on his way. Suddenly a deep voice roused him from his brooding: 'Peldron, I am the oldest dwarf in the world and also the poorest. Please give me something, so that I may buy some food.'

Peldron shook his head. 'No, I won't give you anything,' he said. 'You had better die, so you needn't endure the misery of the world.' And he hurried on without looking back.

Meanwhile Dora, on her way back from the shoemaker, also met the old dwarf, and she too was asked for alms. Like Peldron she refused, but for a different reason.

'I won't give you any money,' she said. 'If you are poor, it's your own fault. The world is so wonderful that I can't be bothered with poor people.' And she skipped along.

With a sigh the old dwarf sat down on a mossy spot wondering what he should do with these two children. One was too sad, the other too gay, and neither would get very far in life that way. Now this ancient dwarf was no ordinary, everyday dwarf; he was a sorcerer, but not an evil one. On the contrary, he wanted people and elves and dwarfs to improve and the world to prosper. He sat there thinking for an hour. Then he rose and slowly walked to the house of Dora's parents.

The day after their meeting in the forest, Dora and Peldron found themselves locked up together in a small cabin. The old dwarf had taken them away to give them a proper training. The great sorcerer's wish was the same as a command,

and even parents dared not disobey it. What were these two to do in the hut? They weren't allowed to go out, nor were they permitted to quarrel. They had to work the whole day long. Those had been the old dwarf's orders. And so Dora worked, made jokes and laughed, and Peldron worked, looked gloomy and felt sad.

Every evening at seven, the old dwarf came to check on their work, and then left again. They wondered how they could possibly get free. There was only one way, and that was to obey the old dwarf in everything.

You can't imagine how difficult it was for Dora to have to look at that long-jawed Peldron all day long; Peldron, Peldron early and late, and never anybody else. But she hadn't much time to talk to him, anyway, even if she had wanted to, because she had to cook (she had learned that from her mother), keep the house clean and in order, and in her 'spare time', if you please, get some spinning done. Peldron, for his part, must chop wood in the enclosed garden, cultivate the garden and cobble shoes into the bargain. At seven in the evening Dora called him to supper, and by that time they were both so tired that they could hardly talk to the old dwarf when he arrived on his nightly visit.

They kept this up for a week. Dora still laughed often, and yet she began to understand that there was a serious side to life. She realised that there were people who had a difficult time, and that it was not asking too much to help such folk when they were in distress, instead of sending them away with some rude words. And Peldron lost a little of his gloom; it even happened, from time to time, that he whistled softly at his work, or grinned when he saw Dora laughing.

On Sunday they were both allowed to come with the old dwarf to chapel in Elves' Village. They paid more attention to the dwarf preacher than they had before, and they felt quite content as they walked back through the shady woods.

'You have been so good,' said the old dwarf, 'that you

may spend the day in the open, just as you used to do. But, mind you, tomorrow you go back to work. You can't go home, and you can't visit your friends.'

Neither thought of running away; they were very glad to be permitted the freedom of the forest, even for one day. All that Sunday they played and had fun, watched the birds and flowers and the blue sky and enjoyed the warm sunshine. Happily they returned to their cabin in the evening, slept until morning, and then went back to work.

The old dwarf made them lead this kind of life for four months. Every Sunday morning they went to chapel, spent the rest of the day in the open, and worked hard the remainder of the week. When the four months were up, the old dwarf one evening took both of them by the hand and walked into the woods with them.

'Look here, children,' he said, 'I am sure that you have often been angry with me. I also think that you must both be longing to go home.'

'Yes,' said Dora; and 'Yes,' echoed Peldron.

'But do you understand that this time has been good for you?'

No, they didn't understand it very well.

'Well, I will explain it,' said the old dwarf. 'I took you here and left you together to teach you that there are other things in this world beside *your* fun, Dora, and *your* gloom, Peldron. You will both get along in life much better than before you came here. Little Dora has become somewhat more serious, and Peldron has cheered up a bit, because you were obliged to make the best of having to live together. I also believe that you like each other better than before. Don't you agree, Peldron?'

'Yes,' said Peldron, 'I like Dora much better now.'

'Well,' said the old dwarf, 'you may go back to your parents. But think often about your stay in the little cabin. Enjoy all the fine things life will bring you, but don't forget the sorrows of others, and try to comfort them. All people, dwarfs and elves can help one another. So be on your way, and don't be cross with me any more. I have done for you what I could, and it was for your own good. Good day, children, till we meet again.'

'Good-bye,' said Dora and Peldron, and off they went to their homes.

Once more the old dwarf sat down in a shady spot. He had but one wish—that he might guide all the children of men into the right path, as he had guided these two.

And truly Dora and Peldron lived happily ever after! Once and for all they had learned the great lesson that people must laugh and weep, each at the right time. Later, much later, when they were grown up, they went to live together in a small house, of their own free will, and Dora did the work inside, and Peldron outside, just as they had when they were very young.

From Stories from the House Behind *by Anne Frank, translated by Michel Mok (World's Work (1913) Ltd.).*

III

NURSERY RHYME STORIES

SEVEN LITTLE GIRLS

Once upon a time there were seven little girls; and each of them was born on a different day of the week.

The eldest little girl was born on a Monday. Her name was Mona, and she was very, very pretty.

The second little girl was born on Tuesday. Her name was Theresa, and she was very graceful and loved dancing.

The third little girl was born on Wednesday, and her name was Wendy She was very delicate, and often ill, and she went about with a sad and woeful face.

The fourth little girl was born on Thursday, and her name was Thora.

The fifth little girl was born on Friday. Her name was Freda, and she had a very kind and loving nature.

The sixth little girl was born on Saturday, and she was called Sandra.

And the seventh little girl was born on Sunday. Her real name was Mary, but everyone called her Sunny, because she was always so happy and gay, like a little ray of sunshine.

Now what happened to these seven little girls when they grew up?

Well, the eldest little girl, Mona, was so pretty that she went in for a beauty competition and won the prize. This prize was a lovely long holiday in another country. So she went away from home. 'That's one gone,' said her mother sadly.

The second little girl, Theresa, was so graceful and danced so well that she became a ballet dancer, and went to a dancing school. So she too went away from home. 'That's two gone,' said the mother sadly.

The third little girl, Wendy, was so delicate that she had to go to hospital. 'That's three gone,' said the mother sadly.

The fourth little girl, Thora, was invited to go and stay with her granny, who lived a long way away. 'That's four gone,' said the mother sadly.

The fifth little girl, Freda, was so kind and loving that a young man asked her to marry him, and so she went away to have a home and children of her own. 'That's five gone,' said the mother sadly.

The sixth little girl, Sandra, wanted to be a nurse, so she went away to learn how to do it in a hospital, and worked very hard. 'That's six gone,' said the mother sadly.

Now there was only the seventh little girl, Sunny, left at home. 'Are you going away too, Sunny?' asked her mother.

'Oh no, Mother,' said Sunny. 'I'm going to stay here with you.' So she stayed at home and helped her mother, and she was so wise and happy and good and gay that everybody loved her. And that is the end of the story of the seven little girls.

Except that here is a rhyme about it:

Monday's child is fair of face;
Tuesday's child is full of grace;
Wednesday's child is full of woe;
Thursday's child has far to go;
Friday's child is loving and giving;
Saturday's child works hard for a living;
But the child that is born on the Sabbath day
Is wise and happy and good and gay.

CROSSPATCH

Crosspatch!
Draw the latch,
Sit by the fire and spin;
Take a cup
And drink it up
And call your neighbours in.

Have you heard that rhyme? And do you know the story of old Mrs. Muggins? That was her real name; but all the people who lived near her called her Crosspatch, because she had such a bad temper, She was always grumbling. If it was a fine day, she said it was too dry; and if it was a wet day, she said it was too damp. And she was specially cross with the two little boys next door, Timmy and Tommy, because she said they made a noise when they were playing in their garden.

One snowy night before Christmas, old Mrs. Muggins was sitting by the fire spinning wool on her spinning-wheel. She had shut the door and drawn the latch, and she felt very cosy. As she sat by the fire, she looked out of the window and saw Timmy and Tommy going by with their toboggan. She knew they were going to the field at the end of the lane where they could toboggan down the hill. They waved and called as they went by, but old Crosspatch didn't wave and smile back. 'Noisy little things!' she thought. 'Well, anyway, I shan't hear them up on the hill.'

After she had been spinning by the fire for quite a long time, she began to feel cold. 'I'll make myself a nice hot cup of cocoa to warm me up,' she thought. So she made herself a cup; and while she was drinking it, she turned on the radio. As it was near Christmas, there were carols being sung, and then someone began to talk about Christmas. 'Do you know what Christmas is?' said a voice. 'It is the time when we stop thinking about ourselves and begin thinking about other people and how we can help them.'

'Huff! Stuff!' said old Crosspatch. But she thought about it, all the same. And then she looked out of the window and saw Timmy and Tommy going past again on their way home. But this time they weren't laughing and waving. Timmy was crying, and Tommy had his arm round his brother's shoulder and was trying to comfort him.

Mrs. Muggins went to the window and opened it.

'What's the matter?' she called.

'Timmy fell off the toboggan and hurt himself,' Tommy called back. 'His leg's bleeding, and Mummy's out shopping.'

'You'd better come in here,' said Mrs. Muggins. And she brought them in by the fire, and tied up Timmy's leg—it wasn't *very* bad—and made them each a hot cup of cocoa with sugar biscuits to eat with it. And while she was doing it, all the crossness went out of her face, and she looked happy and smiling.

Presently they saw the boys' mother going by with her shopping bag, on her way home.

'There goes your mother,' said Mrs. Muggins. 'Now run along home to her.'

'Thank you, Mrs. Muggins,' said Timmy, 'for tying up my leg.'

'Thank you for the cocoa,' said Tommy. And he put his arms round her neck and whispered in her ear, 'I think you look just like Christmas, and we'll never call you Crosspatch any more.'

That night Timmy and Tommy's father came to thank Mrs. Muggins for her kindness to the boys.

'Well,' she said, 'they were my neighbours, and I had to call them in.'

'We were wondering whether you would like to come and have Christmas dinner with us,' said the boys' father.

'Oh, thank you, I'd love to,' said Mrs. Muggins. Nobody had ever asked her to do that before, because she had always been such an old Crosspatch. But she did go to dinner, and they all had a wonderful time, and Mrs. Muggins became a real friend of Timmy and Tommy and their family.

BAA, BAA, BLACK SHEEP

'Baa, baa, black sheep,
Have you any wool?'
'Yes, sir, yes, sir,
Three bags full—
One for my master,
And one for my dame,
But none for the naughty boy
That lives down the lane.'

I expect you know that rhyme. Well, here is a story about it.

There was once a little girl called Jenny, who lived on a farm with her father and mother. Her father was the farmer. One day Jenny came into the kitchen, and saw something very surprising. Her mother's cooking stove had four ovens —one very hot, one just hot, one fairly hot and one nice and cool; and sticking out of the nice and cool oven was a little black woolly head, which said, 'Meh!'

'Oh, Mummy,' said Jenny, 'a little black lamb in the oven!'

'Yes,' said her mother. 'Her mummy the sheep can't feed her, so Daddy brought her in here for us to look after. I put her in the oven to keep her warm. I am just going to give her a bottle—would you like to help?'

'Oh yes,' said Jenny. So her mummy showed her how to give a baby lamb a bottle, and after that Jenny used to look after the lamb, and often gave her her bottle all by herself. Jenny called the lamb Lulu, and she loved her very much. She and her mother took such good care of Lulu that she grew into a great big sheep, with lovely thick black wool. People said they had never seen such fine wool on any sheep.

'When the shearers come to cut the sheep's wool off,' said the farmer's wife, 'I shall keep Lulu's wool separate and have it spun specially, and make something very nice out of it.'

Now down the lane beyond the farm there lived a boy called Jem. He was a rough boy, and not very kind. When Lulu grew too big to be in the farmhouse any more, she was put out in the meadow with the other sheep; and when no one was there to see, Jem used to chase her round and round. And one day he did a really dreadful thing. He threw a stone at her. Luckily it missed; but it might have cut poor Lulu very badly. The farmer's wife was watching out of the window, and she saw what Jem did, but she didn't say anything just then.

Shearing time came, and the men cut the wool off all the sheep with big scissors. It didn't hurt them, and they were very glad to have got rid of their heavy, hot fleeces. Lulu's lovely black wool was kept separate, and the farmer's wife had it spun into balls of wool for her to knit.

One day Jem came to the farm to buy some eggs. He went into the farm kitchen, and there on the table were three paper bags. Jenny was peeping into them.

'Look, Jem', she said. 'Here are three bags full of Lulu's wool.'

'Yes,' said her mother. 'I'm going to knit them into useful things.'

'What are you going to make?' asked Jem.

'First I'm going to make a big pair of socks to go into the farmer's Wellingtons,' said the farmer's wife. 'They will keep his toes warm on cold days. And then I'm going to make a middle-sized pair for myself. And then I'm going to make a smaller pair.'

'Who will they be for?' asked Jenny and Jem together.

'They will be,' said the farmer's wife, 'for the person who has been kindest to Lulu. I wonder who that is.'

Jem looked down at his feet. He knew he hadn't been kind to Lulu. 'Jenny had better have them,' he said.

So you see, there was one bag full for the master—that was the farmer; and there was one bag full for the dame—that was the farmer's wife; but there was none for the naughty boy that lived down the lane—and that was Jem. The song doesn't say anything about Jenny, but she got her nice warm socks all the same; and that is the happy ending of the story.

FOR WANT OF A NAIL

This is the story of two king's sons. One was called Prince Primus because he was the eldest, and the other was called Prince Secundus, because he was born second. And they both wanted to be king. But it was very difficult to decide which of them should be king, because they were twins—only Prince Primus was born just a little bit sooner than Prince Secundus. Prince Secundus said such a little bit of time didn't matter, but Prince Primus said it did, and he ought to be king.

They argued and argued and argued, and at last they said, 'Well, we shall just have to fight about it.' So Prince Primus gathered an army, and Prince Secundus gathered an army, and they all camped facing each other on the plain.

Such a commotion there was that night, with all the troops getting ready for the battle next day—such a sharpening of swords and polishing of armour and grooming of horses. Prince Primus was sitting in his tent making his plans for the battle, and he sent for one of his knights called Sir Scudamore. 'You have a very fast horse, haven't you?' he asked him.

'Yes, Your Highness,' said the knight, 'the fastest in your army.'

'Then you shall be my messenger tomorrow,' said the prince. 'You shall take my orders to the commanders and tell them when to go into battle.'

'Very well, Your Highness,' said Sir Scudamore, and he went off to get ready for the job. He looked at his sword and his shield and his spear and all the rest of his armour, and that was all right. Then he looked at his saddle and his bridle and the rest of his horse's harness, and that was all right. Then he looked at his horse, and that was all right too. And the last thing he did was to pick up his horse's hoofs and look to see that the horseshoes were all well nailed on. And they were quite all right too. So then he went off to bed and had a good sleep.

Meanwhile, Prince Secundus had been sitting in *his* tent and making *his* plans for the battle too. And he sent for one of his knights called Sir Dumbledore. 'You have a very fast horse, haven't you?' he asked.

'Yes, Your Highness,' said the knight, 'the fastest in your army.'

'Then you shall be my messenger tomorrow,' said Prince Secundus, 'and tell my commanders when to go into battle.'

'Very good, Your Highness,' said Sir Dumbledore, and he went off to get ready for the job. He looked at his sword and his shield and his spear and the rest of his armour, and that was all right. Then he looked at his saddle and his bridle and the rest of his horse's harness, and that was all right. Then he looked at his horse, and that was all right too. But when he picked up his horse's hoofs, he saw that there was a nail missing in one of the shoes. Now Sir Dumbledore was a lazy knight, and did not want to bother to take his horse to have a new nail hammered in. 'One nail doesn't matter,' he said. So he too went off to bed and had a good sleep.

Next morning in the two camps there was such a blowing of trumpets and cooking of breakfasts and arming of knights and harnessing of horses, till at last both armies were ready for the battle.

'Give my commanders the order to charge,' said Prince Primus to Sir Scudamore. And off he rode.

'Give my commanders the order to charge,' said Prince Secundus to Sir Dumbledore. And off he rode too. So there they were, both galloping along at full speed to tell the two armies to charge. But that nail was missing in Sir Dumble-dore's horse's shoe; and presently that hoof hit a stone, and that loosened another nail, and then another and another, till the shoe came right off. The horse stumbled, and Sir Dumbledore shot over its head and on to the ground. He got up, though it was very difficult in his heavy armour, and tried to mount his horse again; but it was too late—Sir Scudamore had reached Prince Primus's army and given his message to the commanders.

'Charge!' they shouted, and down they came on to Prince Secundus's army, who weren't expecting them. They turned and ran away, and that was the end of the battle. And that was how Prince Secundus lost the kingdom, and how Prince Primus won it.

You may sometimes hear people say a rhyme about all this:

> For want of a nail, the shoe was lost;
> For want of a shoe, the horse was lost;
> For want of a horse, the rider was lost;
> For want of a rider, the battle was lost;
> For want of a battle, the kingdom was lost;
> And all for want of a horse-shoe nail!

And now you will know something about it.

THE STORY OF THE LITTLE CROOKED MAN

I expect you know the rhyme:

> There was a crooked man,
> And he walked a crooked mile;
> He found a crooked sixpence
> Upon a crooked stile.
> He bought a crooked cat,
> Who caught a crooked mouse;
> And they all lived together
> In a little crooked house.

But don't think the little man was always crooked. Oh dear me, no. He was as straight as you or I when this story begins. His name was Jeremy Juggins, and he lived by himself in a pretty little cottage. And that wasn't crooked either in the beginning. By no means. For Jeremy had built it himself, and he had taken the greatest pains to see that the walls were straight and the roof put on just so. It was after that that the crookedness began.

It all happened one market day. Jeremy was upstairs, looking at himself in the looking glass as he tied the smart tie which he always wore to market, when he happened to glance out of the window, and there he saw old Mrs. Tibbetts, who lived a little way down the lane, setting off for town, carrying her basket. The basket looked very heavy, and Jeremy knew that it was loaded with the eggs and butter and cheese which the old dame was taking to market.

'Run downstairs, Jeremy,' whispered a kind little voice inside him, 'and help Mrs. Tibbetts to carry that heavy basket.'

'Don't want to,' grumbled Jeremy; and he stood and watched the old lady as she went along the field path through the meadow till she came to a stile, and with much difficulty climbed over it. Then she disappeared from view, and Jeremy thought that he had better set out too. But he didn't feel very comfortable inside himself—he still felt he ought to have helped Mrs. Tibbetts. He wandered along through the field, and swished at the nettles in the ditch with his stick, and threw stones into Farmer Giles's pond. He took so long in his wanderings that by the time he got to the stile he had walked quite a mile, and a crooked mile at that. And by this time there was something crooked inside Jeremy too.

As he climbed over the little stile, which was made of crooked knobbly bits of wood, he saw lying on the top of it something bright and shining. He picked it up, and saw that it was a sixpenny bit—but rather a funny one, for it was all bent and battered.

'Why, it's Mrs. Tibbetts's lucky sixpence,' he thought. 'She showed it to me only the other day.'

The kind little voice inside him said, 'Put it in your pocket, and when you see Mrs. Tibbetts at the market, give it back to her.'

But the crooked thoughts in Jeremy's head ran like this: 'Silly old woman! She ought to look after her money better. If she's so careless as to lose it, I shall keep it myself.' So on he went, thinking his crooked thoughts, till he came to the market town.

It was quite a long way, and by the time he had got there, he was very hungry and thirsty, and he thought he would go into an inn for some food and drink. He put his hand in his pocket. Oh dear! He had left all his money at home! He had nothing at all but the little crooked sixpence. He went to the bun stall, but the bun lady wouldn't take it for buns. He went to the lemonade shop, but they wouldn't take it either. And when he offered it to the ice-cream man, the man just laughed.

'Keep your sixpence,' he said. 'It's as crooked as yourself.'

'I'm not crooked,' said Jeremy.

'Look in the glass,' said the ice-cream man, as he trundled his cart away.

Jeremy sauntered over to a shop window, and there he saw in the glass—what? Not the straight, upstanding Jeremy he was used to, but a little bent old man with a crooked face. The sight shocked him so much that he didn't want to go on looking at things in the market. He decided to go home.

So back he went, over the fields, and the little stile, till he came to Farmer Giles's pond. And there were some cruel boys just going to throw a cat into the water to see if she could swim.

'You mustn't do that,' he cried. 'Here, give me the poor thing.'

'She's mine,' said one of the boys. 'You'll have to pay me for her.'

'This is all I've got,' said Jeremy, holding out the crooked sixpence. 'It's a *lucky* sixpence,' he added.

'All right,' said the boy, and he took the sixpence, and handed over the cat, who went gladly with her new friend.

A little farther, and Jeremy was back at his own house again. But oh—what a shock! Instead of the neat little house, with its nice straight walls, there was a tumbledown shack, with its chimney pots leaning one way and its roof leaning the other. Even the path to the porch was twisty instead of straight. Jeremy opened the crooked door and walked into his crooked kitchen. He sat down on his favourite stool, whose legs had suddenly become twisted, and he looked at his new pet the cat. He saw that it too was all crooked.

'Everything seems crooked today,' he cried. 'What can be the matter?' And he felt very, very miserable. As he sat there, listening to the ticking of the clock, he thought it sounded like words. Yes—listen!

'Jer-em-y! Jer-em-y! Put it straight! Put it straight!'

'Put what straight?' he cried. He jumped up and tried to straighten the pictures, which were hanging all crooked on the crooked walls. But no—they hung as crookedly as ever. And still the clock went on: 'Put it straight! Put it straight! Say you're sor-ry! Put it straight!'

'But how can I?' cried Jeremy. 'It's too late to carry Mrs. Tibbetts's basket now. And I haven't got her crooked sixpence any more.'

Just at that very moment he heard voices outside. He looked out, and saw some boys—the ones who had sold him the cat. A sudden idea came to him. He went over to a drawer, and crooked though it was, managed to get it open. Inside was his money. He took out a bright new sixpence.

Then he went to the crooked window, and called out, 'Boy! Here's a nice new sixpence for that old bent one.'

The boy came running up, glad to change the coins. 'Well, that's one thing put straight,' thought Jeremy, but still everything was crooked in the little crooked house, and still Jeremy felt very, very sad.

The cat came and rubbed her crooked back against his knees, for she felt very sorry for him. She even managed to catch a mouse, and brought it to him to cheer him up. But the mouse was crooked too, and poor Jeremy felt sadder than ever.

And still the clock was ticking away: 'Give it back! Give it back! Say you're sor-ry! Give it back!'

'I WILL!' said Jeremy loudly. He got up and took his stick —crooked, of course—opened the crooked door, and hobbled down his twisty path to his twisty gate. Down the lane he went to Mrs. Tibbetts's house, and knocked on her green painted door. She opened it, and Jeremy held out the sixpence.

'Mrs. Tibbetts, ma'am,' he stammered, 'I brought this back.'

'Why, bless my soul,' said the old lady, 'wherever did you find it?'

'On the stile,' said Jeremy. He was just going away when he thought, 'I haven't really put it straight.' So he said, 'I knew it was yours, but I didn't give it back to you. And I know I ought to have carried your basket, and I'm very sorry—o-o-o-oh!' For Jeremy suddenly felt his back go straight, and when he looked down at the cat, which had followed him and was rubbing against his legs, he saw that it had a straight back too. Home he ran to his little cottage, and there it was, as straight and square as ever. He hurried inside, and there was the little mouse, straight and happy, playing a little game all by itself in front of the fire. It ran into its hole when it saw Jeremy and the cat, and peeped out at them with bright beady eyes.

And the old clock in the corner ticked away, and said, 'Well done you! Well done you! Now keep straight. Now keep straight.' And Jeremy promised that he would.

And that is the story of the little crooked man.

John Cromwell

IV

NATURE

THE BUSY BEE

The busy bee had been working hard all day. She had flown from flower to flower, sipping a little honey from each. When she had gathered all she could carry, back she flew to the beehive and put it in the honey store. Then off she flew again for more. Back and forth, to and fro she went, till the sun began to go down and the evening came on. Soon she must go back to the hive for the night. But just then she saw another flower—a big red tulip. 'There will be some fine honey in there,' she thought; and in she went. There was so much honey that she was quite a long time gathering it; and when at last she turned to go out, she found that she could not. The tulip had shut up for the night. Its satiny petals were all pressed together, and there was no way out.

At first the busy bee fussed and bumbled and tried to find a way; but at last she grew so tired that she fell asleep, there inside the tulip. It was a lovely soft bed, and smelt so sweet that the little bee had a wonderful sleep.

At last morning came, and the tulip flower opened up again in the morning sunshine. Out popped the busy bee, and away she flew to the hive. What an adventure she had had! It was a very exciting story to tell the other bees, before she flew off again to gather more honey in this new day which had just begun.

THE HAPPY LITTLE TORTOISE

A true story

Jerry was a little tortoise. But when this story begins, he was not happy at all. Tortoises like to crawl about on grass and eat green growing things. But there was no grass where Jerry was, and no green growing things. He was on the London pavements with a man who wanted to sell him. He called out to the passers-by, 'Buy a tortoise! Buy a fine tortoise!'

A lady came by, and when she saw poor little Jerry she stopped. 'Oh, the poor little tortoise!' she said. 'He does look miserable.'

'You buy him, lady,' said the man who wanted to sell him. 'Then he'll eat all the slugs and beetles in your garden for you.'

'But I haven't got a garden,' said the lady. She didn't tell the man that tortoises don't eat slugs and beetles—only green growing things. She stood still and thought. Then she said, 'I know what I'll do.' She gave the man some money, and he put Jerry into her hand. 'Oh, whatever is happening now?' thought poor Jerry.

Then the lady called a taxi-cab, and got in with Jerry. 'Take me to Kensington Gardens,' she said. So the taxi-man drove off, and the lady put Jerry on the seat. It was softer than the pavement, but it still wasn't green grass. Then, when they came to the gardens, the lady told the taxi-man to stop. She got out and paid him, and then she walked on to the grass and very gently put Jerry down on it. He sniffed around—grass at last, and things to eat! He started to gobble the green growing things, and the lady watched him, feeling so glad that he was in the place where he belonged. The taxi-driver drove off.' What a funny lady!' he was thinking. But Jerry was scuttling along as fast as his legs would carry him—but that was not very fast, you know—and at last he was a really happy little tortoise.

HIS FIRST FLIGHT

A little baby woodpecker poked his head out of the hole in which he lived. His little, beady eyes took in everything around him. He saw the squirrel, the magpie, the jay and all the inhabitants of the world. With a flutter of wings he gained a small branch jutting out below the nest. He ruffled his rather dull plumage; his body quivered all over; he was plucking up his courage to do something. He was trying to make up his mind to fly. He sat there wondering if he dared.

Suddenly there was a loud report of a shot-gun. In sheer fright he toppled off his perch; he fell about three feet; and then, as if by magic, with a whirr of wings, he soared to the top of a beech tree.

He sat on a branch, wondering what had happened. He couldn't understand it; one minute he was sitting outside his nest, and the next moment he was on top of a beech tree! Then it slowly dawned upon him. (He could fly!) A great surge of excitement flowed through him, and, spreading his little wings again, he flew away.

R. P. King (age 13): From Life Through Young Eyes, *a collection of children's writings (Dolphin Publishing Co., 1960).*

THE STREAM

This is the story of a stream. He was a very tiny little stream to begin with—just a little trickle of water coming out of a hill. But he said to himself, 'I must get to the sea,' and he began to run and run, always downhill.

But presently he came to a lot of big, hard stones. 'You shan't go on,' said the rocks. 'I shall,' said the stream. So he ran and he ran, always down the hill, and he ran right round those big stones and away down the hill. And all the time he was saying to himself, 'I must get to the sea.'

Presently he came to a big hole in the ground, and into it he fell. Underneath the ground there was a dark, dark tunnel, and along it the little stream had to run, always down the hill. 'You shan't go on,' said the tunnel. 'I shall,' said the stream. And he ran and he ran, always downhill, till at last he ran out from underground into the bright sunlight again. And all the time he was saying to himself, 'I must get to the sea.'

But the place where he had come out was a very flat place, and the little stream found it very hard to run, because he could only run downhill. 'You shan't go on,' said the flat place. 'I shall,' said the stream. And he ran and he ran until he had made himself a channel to run in. And all the time he was saying to himself, 'I must get to the sea.'

Then winter came on, and the frost took hold of everything with his icy fingers. He took the water of the stream and turned nearly all of it to ice, so that it couldn't move. 'You shan't go on,' said the frost. 'I shall,' said the stream. Deep down under the ice he still had a little trickle of water that was not frozen. So he ran and he ran, always downhill, till at last the spring came, and the warm weather melted the ice and all his water was free to move again. And all the time he was saying to himself, 'I must get to the sea.'

At last he came to a great river, and his water ran into the river water and got all mixed up in it. 'Oh dear,' said the stream. 'I shall never get to the sea now.'

'Yes, you will,' said the big river kindly. 'You come with me, and I will take you there.'

So the stream was swept along by the big river, and boats sailed on him, and he saw children fishing on the river banks, and other wonderful things. And at last one day the river grew wider and wider, so that there were no bank, at all, only water, water everywhere. And that water was salt. And all the time the stream was saying, 'I must get to the sea—I must get to the sea—why, I'm THERE!'

SAYING 'THANK YOU'

A boy was once very thirsty, and he went to the tap for a drink. He drank the good cold water. 'Thank you, Tap,' he said.

'Don't thank me,' said the tap. 'I'm glad to help you, but I only make the water run.'

'Well, then, thank you, Water,' said the boy. 'You have been very kind to me.'

'Don't thank me,' said the water. 'It is the spring on the hillside which sends me out for you to drink.'

'I'll thank the spring then,' said the boy.

'Don't thank me,' said the spring. 'I could not run without the dew and the rain.'

'I'll thank the dew and rain, then,' said the boy.

'Don't thank us,' said the dew and the rain. 'It is the sun which draws us up into the air to fall down again on the earth.'

'Thank you, Mr. Sun,' said the boy. But the sun said, 'Don't thank me. I drew the water up out of the ocean.'

'Thank you, Ocean,' said the boy. But the ocean said, 'No, don't thank me. Thank Him who made me, and the sun, and the dew and rain, and the spring, and the water, and helped men to make the tap.' So at last the boy knew whom he should thank; and he said thank you to God.

A prose version of a poem called 'TO WHOM SHALL WE GIVE THANKS?'—*The Story of Water by an anonymous author. From* The Golden Pathway, *Vol. II. International University Society.*

ADVENTURES OF A FISH

I am a fish. I belong to the Perch family. I live in a lake which has several small islands in it. One day I was swimming along with the rest of our tribe, when suddenly I saw a real, luscious, juicy worm dangling in front of me. I rushed at it, but it wasn't there; it had moved a yard above. I rushed at it again and started to swallow it, when suddenly I felt something like a tough, thin piece of weed in my mouth. Ow! Something was pricking my gills. Quick as a trout, I spat it out; and then I saw that a thin piece of gut was attached to the worm.

I had heard of these. The worm had a hook in it. Some beastly human was trying to catch me and take me to his house. 'Don't eat that worm,' I bubbled (fish always bubble when they speak), pointing to it with my starboard fin.

I decided I had better go away. I swam hard till I came to the mouth of the river, and then I decided that I would make a great journey up the river and see if there was anything interesting there. I set out slowly. After about two miles I came to a large, very deep pool. Just as I went round a corner, a huge pike rushed at me and started to chase me. I quickly stuck up my spikes, but still the pike chased. He chased me round and round till I was quite tired, and then suddenly I dived quickly down near the bottom of the pool. It was quite dark there, but I managed to see a small cranny at the side, so I sped straight into it. The pike, who had been following obstinately, was not quick enough to intercept this move. He dashed past me and banged his head on a jutting-out piece of rock. He stayed drifting for a second, but then I saw that he was watching me, so I raced to the bottom end of the pool, shot down the river, and arrived back at the lake.

I had still to find my tribe, though, so I slowly went round the lake. At last I found them, just finishing off a large shoal of minnows.

'Ha! Ha!' they said, 'that's what becomes of people who think themselves too clever and go off on their own.' My fins went green; so did my face (that's a fish blushing).

'I'm sorry,' I murmured, 'I won't do it again.' I did not, you can be sure, because I like minnows—and I do not like pike.

W. A. Willink (age 11): From Life Through Young Eyes *(Dolphin Publishing Co., 1960).*

THE BEST NEST

This is the story of a little fairy girl called Dawn.

Dawn had a wood. Nearly all the birds who lived in the wood were her friends. She used to take care of the baby birds while their mothers went off to the stream to have a bathe or a drink. . . . The thrushes were very fond of bathing. They would often bring their babies to Dawn, and ask her to look after them while they went away to the stream. The baby thrushes were very solemn little birds. As the thrushes are the best singers in the wood next to the nightingales, they thought rather a lot of themselves. They were only allowed to play with their cousins the missel thrushes.

The missel thrush was very proud of himself, because he always knew when bad weather was coming. He sang a loud song about it, and when the other birds heard his song they would hurry back to their nests and babies.

'None of the birds seem to know how to build nests except our family,' said the thrush to Dawn. '*We* put mud at the bottom, and we make them so strong that they can float in water.'

'I don't see any use in having a nest that can float,' said a chaffinch. 'I make my nest soft and cosy, and build it in a hidden spot where all the hawks and shrikes can't find it.'

'Well, our nests are so strong that we can use the same nest again next spring,' said the thrush.

The chaffinch went away and called his cousins, the bullfinch, the greenfinch and the goldfinch.

'We want you to say which of us builds the best nest,' they said to Dawn. Dawn said that before she could tell she must first go and visit their nests.

'You must come and see mine first,' said the bullfinch. His nest was in a hawthorn bush. It was made of twigs and roots to hold the twigs together. Dawn did not like to tell the bullfinch, but she did not think it a very good nest. Then she went to see the greenfinch's nest. His nest was much prettier, and was made of moss and hairs and feathers. He was rather a shy, quiet bird, and not so proud as the bullfinch. Then Dawn went to see the chaffinch's nest. It was even prettier than the greenfinch's. One of the babies had hopped out of the nest and was sitting on the bough close by.

'I have to make my nest all alone,' said the mother chaffinch. 'My husband is too lazy to help me, but he always helps me to feed the babies.'

'Your babies look very fat and beautiful,' said Dawn.

'Yes, we give them lots of insects. We ourselves are very fond of dead nettle seeds, but we never give the babies anything but tiny insects.'

'We love thistle-down seeds,' cried the lovely little goldfinch. 'But come and see my nest.'

When Dawn saw the little goldfinch's nest, she knew who she would give the prize to. It was such a beautiful little round nest, with five pale blue tiny eggs, just spotted at one end with brown spots. The bullfinch puffed himself out when Dawn said she must give the prize to the goldfinch. He went away and was very sulky.

From From Dawn to Twilight *by Nell Parsons*
(Robert Culley).

THE LITTLE GREY HORSE

One day, in the fresh green meadow at the back of Apple Orchard Farm, a little grey horse was born. He was a funny, ugly little fellow, with his awkward long legs; but he grew and he grew, and by the time two years had passed he had grown into a lovely little horse, and had been given the name of Grey Knight.

Life was great fun there in the meadow, with only old Betty the mare to keep him company. Betty had been in all sorts of places and done all sorts of work, and had now grown too old and worn out to go anywhere or to do anything. They would run races round the field, and the Grey Knight would pretend to go lame, and let old Betty outdistance him; then he would toss his head and throw up his tail, and like a flash he was past old Betty with a flick of his heels in the air.

When they were tired, they would lie down together in the shade of the trees, and Betty would tell stories of her young days, of the masters she had had, and the places she had been in . . . and always she would finish her story— 'And then the old motto carried me through: "Do your work and don't fuss." ' She told her stories so often that Grey Knight knew them by heart, and when she got near the end he would jump up and say, 'Yes, I know the rest, Betty—"Do your work and don't fuss." '

Then the time came for Grey Knight to work. His master rode him out hunting with the hounds. By this time he was more handsome than ever and he felt more than a little proud of himself. He could not help overhearing the fine things people said about him, and when he had jumped a difficult fence or an awkward stream, and his master patted his neck, he felt *much more* than a little proud of himself. After such a day, if he saw old Betty, he would tell her all about the admiration and praise he had had. Only Betty never seemed to think much of it. She would rub her nose against the stable partition and say in her quiet way, 'Well, do your work and don't fuss.'

Then changes came to Apple Orchard Farm, and Grey Knight was sold—sold to go to London to be a policeman's horse. It was not at all nice at first. There were no green fields to roll in, and no cold streams to bathe in, and he had to spend his days in the streets, which were full of motor-cars and buses, motor-bikes and taxis, that smelt horribly, and made all sorts of horrid noises. There were so many things that Grey Knight had to learn not to do, and they were not easy things: to stand with your nose on a barrow full of apples and not eat any of them, to push people back without stepping on their toes, to move quietly and slowly when motors and buses were flying past you every way.

Sometimes there would be bigger crowds than usual in the streets, and very noisy crowds, everyone shouting and waving things, and even the Grey Knight used to find it hard not to be nervous and afraid. Then his master would bend over and pat his neck and whisper in his ear, and the words of old Betty would come back to him: 'Do your work and don't fuss.'

From Stories from an Old Garden *by William J. May (Allenson & Co. Ltd.) Slightly shortened and adapted.*

V

MYTHS AND LEGENDS

THE DOG IN THE MANGER

There was once a dog who was looking for a nice soft place to sleep. He came into a stable and saw the manger full of hay.

'Oh,' he said, 'this will make a nice bed.' And in he jumped and settled down comfortably. Presently the oxen whose stable it was came in from their work, very tired and hungry, and went to the manger to eat the hay. But the dog growled and snapped at them, and would not let them come near it.

'What a selfish dog!' said one of the oxen to his companion. 'He cannot eat the hay himself, and yet he refuses to let us eat it who can.'

THE BLIND MAN AND THE LAME MAN

A blind man and a lame man were once walking along a road when they came to a part which was very bumpy and uneven.

'Please,' said the blind man to the lame man, 'will you help me over this difficult piece of road, for I cannot see where the bumps are.'

'How can I help you?' said the lame man. 'I am so lame that I can hardly get along myself.' Then he had a thought. 'I will tell you what we will do,' he said. 'You shall carry me on your back. Then I can tell you where the bad places are, and you can carry me over them. Your feet will be my feet, and my eyes will be your eyes.'

'What a splendid plan!' said the blind man. 'In that way we can help each other.' So that is what they did; and they got along famously.

THE MOUSE AND THE WEASEL

There was once a hungry little mouse who found a basket of corn. He climbed inside it and began to eat. He stuffed and he stuffed, while his little body grew fatter and fatter; and at last he had had enough. But still he went on eating.

Then he tried to get out; but he could not. The hole was too small for his fat body to pass through. And there he had to stay, groaning and crying because he was a prisoner.

A friend of his, a weasel, heard his cries and came to see what was the matter. But there was nothing he could do to help the greedy little mouse out of his prison. 'I'm afraid you will just have to stay there, my friend,' said he, 'and starve till you are thin. You will never get out till you are as small as you were when you went in.'

THE TREASURE IN THE FIELD

A farmer once said to his sons, 'My children, when I die, I am leaving you a great treasure, which lies buried in my field.'

Not long afterwards he died, and the sons said to each other, 'We must go and dig in the field and find this great treasure which our father has left us.' So they set to work with their spades and hoes and ploughs and harrows and every farm tool they could find. They dug and ploughed and harrowed and hoed, and turned up the soil over and over again; but no rich treasure did they find.

But when harvest time came, the land yielded a far finer crop than ever before, because of all the hard work they had put into it. This crop they sold for a great deal of money, enough to keep them all in comfort; and then they realised that there had indeed been a great treasure hidden in the field, and that they had had to dig hard and long to find it.

THE ANT AND THE PIGEON

A little ant was very thirsty, and went to the water to drink. But she leaned over too far, and fell in.

'Oh, help me, help me!' she cried, as she struggled in the water. A pigeon happened to fly past and heard her cries.

'I will help you,' she said. She flew to a bush, picked off a leaf and let it fall into the water near the ant. The ant climbed on to the leaf, and it floated her safely to the edge of the water.

'Oh, thank you, thank you!' cried the ant to the pigeon. 'You have saved my life. I hope that some day I shall be able to save yours.'

The pigeon laughed, for she did not see how this could ever happen. But one day a bird-catcher came along and was going to set a trap under the tree where the pigeon was sitting. This was the little ant's chance. She ran up and stung the man sharply in the foot. He jumped and dropped the trap, and the pigeon, hearing the noise, flew safely away.

THE MICE AND THE CAT

A number of mice once lived in a house. In the same house lived a very large and very fierce cat; and she chased and caught so many of the mice that she made their lives a misery to them.

At last they held a meeting to discuss what could be done to save the lives of those who were left. Some of the mice said one thing, and some said another; but they could not agree on any plan.

Then one of the mice said, 'I know what we will do. We will tie a bell round the neck of the cat. Then we shall hear her coming, and be able to get away before she catches us.'

The other mice thought that this was a splendid plan; they were delighted with it, until a wise old mouse said,

'Your plan is a good one; but there is something you have forgotten.'

'What is that?' said the mice.

'Who,' asked the old mouse, 'is going to tie the bell round the neck of the cat?'

And to that question the mice had no answer.

THE BUNDLE OF STICKS

A man once had a family of sons who were always quarrelling among themselves. One day he decided that he would show them how foolish and dangerous this quarrelling was.

'Bring me a bundle of sticks,' he said.

So the bundle was brought, and the father gave it to his eldest son, and asked him to break it in pieces. But though he tried with all his strength, he could not do it.

'Now you try,' he said to his second son; but he could not do it either. Each of the sons tried in turn, but none of them could break the bundle of sticks.

Then the father untied the bundle, and gave one of the sticks to each of his sons.

'Now break the sticks,' he said; and they all broke them easily.

'You see, my sons,' said their father, 'if an enemy should come and find you all quarrelling among yourselves, he would be able to overcome you easily; but if you are all of one mind, he will not be able to harm you, any more than you could break that bundle of sticks.'

THE BOY WHO CRIED 'WOLF!'

There was once a shepherd boy who watched his flock of sheep on a hillside. In those days there were wild beasts, such as wolves, in the forests, and it was the shepherd's duty to keep his flock safe from them.

One day the boy thought he would have some fun; and

he began to call out 'Wolf! Wolf!' The men working in the fields heard him, and they came running to his help, thinking that a wolf must be attacking the sheep. But when they reached the flock, the boy laughed at them, and said that it had only been a joke. After that he often called out 'Wolf!' just to see the men come running up the hillside.

But then one day a wolf really did come. 'Wolf! Wolf!' cried the boy; but the men in the fields shrugged their shoulders and went on working. 'It's only that boy again,' they said. 'We aren't going to be caught by his tricks this time.' Meanwhile the wolf was leaping among the sheep and worrying them, and the foolish boy could do nothing to save his flock.

THE LION AND THE MOUSE

A lion was once asleep in the forest, when a mouse ran over his nose and woke him up. He sprang up in anger, caught the mouse and was just about to kill him, when the mouse squeaked out, 'Oh, Mr. Lion, spare my life, and one day I will repay your kindness.'

The lion laughed scornfully. 'Ha! Ha!' he said. 'How could a little scrap like you help me?' But he let the mouse go.

Some time afterwards hunters came into the forest. They laid a trap for the lion, and caught him in a net made of ropes. There he lay, all tied up and roaring with rage. The little mouse heard his roar.

'That sounds like my friend the lion,' he said. 'And it sounds as if he was in trouble. I will go and see.' So he scuttled along through the forest, and there lay the lion all trussed up with cords.

'This is my chance to repay the lion's kindness,' thought the little mouse; and he set to work to gnaw away at the cords. Soon the net began to give way, and at last the lion was free.

'You see,' said the mouse to the lion, 'you were wrong when you laughed at me because I said I would help you one day. But now you know that even a mouse can help a lion.'

THE MAN ON THE MOUNTAIN

A man was once travelling in the mountains, and was going along a narrow path, when he came to a place where a huge rock had rolled down into the path and blocked it up. The man tried to move it, but he could not shift the heavy stone. Then he tried to climb over it, or squeeze round it, but that was impossible too.

At last, tired out with trying, he sat down against the rock. 'What shall I do?' he thought. 'When night comes in this lonely place I shall be quite alone, with nothing to eat or drink and no weapon if wild animals attack me.'

Presently he heard footsteps, and along came another traveller. He, like the first one, tried every way he could think of to get past the rock; but he had to give it up too. Then came another traveller, and another, until there were quite a number; but no one could move the rock.

At last one said to the others, 'Brothers, let us pray to our Father in heaven; it may be He will help us.' So they did so. And when they had prayed, the man who had said, 'Let us pray,' said, 'Brothers, we could not move the stone alone; but perhaps we could do it if we all pushed together.'

They then got up and all put their shoulders to the rock, and it moved aside, and they were able to go past it and continue their journey.

Retold from a story on Comradeship by
F. R. de Lammenais in Words of a Believer.

THE HARE AND THE TORTOISE

One day a hare, the quickest runner among the animals, met a slow old tortoise plodding along.

'You old slowcoach!' she laughed. 'Can't you go any faster than that?'

'Will you have a race with me,' said the tortoise, 'and see which of us gets to the winning post first?'

'Of course I will,' said the hare. 'And I shall certainly win.' So off they went. Of course the hare soon left the tortoise far behind. She thought the race was a great joke; and when she had gone half-way, she began to play, nibble the grass and practise big jumps. Presently she began to feel tired. 'I will have a little nap,' she thought. 'Even if the tortoise does go past me when I am asleep, I can easily catch him up again when I wake up.' So she lay down in a shady spot and fell fast asleep.

Meanwhile the tortoise was coming slowly but steadily along. He did not stop to eat, or to rest, or to sleep. He just kept on and on. He passed the hare where she lay asleep, and went quietly on towards the winning post.

Suddenly the hare woke up. 'I must have slept too long,' she cried. 'Where is that tortoise? I must catch him up.' Off she ran; but the tortoise was nowhere to be seen. On and on ran the hare till she came to the winning post; and there was the tortoise, already arrived and waiting for her.

Slow and sure wins the race.

THE LOST DUCKLING

Long ago a good and kind man called Saint Bartholomew lived in a place where there were many pools of water. On these pools lived flocks of ducks and geese, which ate the food they found in the water.

One day Saint Bartholomew was sitting on a green bank when he felt something pulling at his coat—tug, tug. He looked down and saw that a duck had caught hold of his coat with her beak and was pulling at it.

'What is the matter, Mother Duck?' asked Saint

Bartholomew. But of course the duck could not tell him. She just kept on tugging.

'Do you want me to come with you?' asked Saint Bartholomew; and he got up. The duck let go of his coat. 'Quack! Quack!' she said, and off she waddled, quacking all the way. Saint Bartholomew went after her, till she came to a steep bank. The mother duck went to the edge and looked over.

'Quack! Quack!' she said. So Saint Bartholomew looked over too. Below the bank was a deep hollow, and at the side of this hollow there was a ledge, and on the ledge was a little duckling. It had fallen over, and couldn't get up again. Its mother could not help it, so she had gone to the man whom she knew to be so good and kind to get him to help her.

'All right, Mother Duck,' he said. 'I'll soon fetch your baby up for you.' He climbed down into the hollow and very gently lifted the little duckling up and put it on the top.

'Quack! Quack! QUACK!' said the mother duck, which was her way of saying, 'Thank you.' Then off she went happily with her baby, and Saint Bartholomew went back to sit on his grassy bank again.

THE WOODMAN AND HIS AXE

A woodman was one day cutting down a tree by the side of a river. By chance he let go of his axe, and it fell into the water and sank to the bottom. The woodman was very sad, for he had no money to buy another.

But the god Mercury came to help him, as he sat grieving on the bank.

'I will get your axe back for you,' he said; and he dived down to the bottom of the river and brought up an axe. But it was made of gold.

'Is this your axe?' he asked.

'Oh no,' said the woodman. 'My axe is made of iron.'

Again Mercury dived into the river, and again he brought up an axe. But this time it was made of shining silver.

'Is this your axe?' he asked.

'Oh no,' said the woodman. 'My axe is made of iron.'

So a third time Mercury dived into the river; and this time he brought up the woodman's own axe.

'Ah, that is mine,' said the woodman gratefully.

'You are an honest fellow,' said Mercury. 'You shall have the gold and silver axes as well as a reward.'

The woodman told his companions what had happened to him; and one of them thought that he too would like a gold and silver axe. So he too went to cut down a tree by the river, and let his axe fall into it. The god Mercury came to him too and offered to fetch it back for him. Again he dived, and brought up a golden axe.

'Is this your axe?' he asked the second woodman.

'Yes, it is,' said he eagerly.

'You are a liar,' said Mercury, 'and to punish you, you shall not have your own axe back again, let alone the gold and silver ones.'

THE NEST IN THE HOOD

Have you a hood on your coat? Big people sometimes have them too, and there was once a man who had a lovely warm one. His name was Saint Malo, and he wore a long, long coat with this nice warm hood to put over his head when it was cold. Saint Malo was a good and kind man, and he specially loved all the birds and beasts.

Saint Malo had a little house, and outside it he had a little garden where he loved to grow pretty flowers and good fresh vegetables. One day he was working in his garden on a very warm day. He grew hot, and took off his warm hood and hung it on a branch for coolness.

Now it happened that a little jenny wren was looking for a nice safe place to make a nest. As she flew about looking, she saw the hood, and flew inside it. 'This is just the place,' she thought, 'so warm and cosy.' So she and her husband fetched grass and moss and made a soft nest, and then she went inside and laid her eggs.

When evening came, it grew chilly, and Saint Malo wanted his hood. He took it off the branch, and then—what a surprise! Out flew a little bird. He guessed what had happened. He put his hand in and felt the grass and moss and a little warm egg. So he hung the hood back on the branch.

'There you are, little wren,' he said. 'You need my hood more than I do.' So little jenny wren flew in again and sat on her eggs till they hatched, and baby wrens came out. She and her husband fed the babies till they grew up and flew away. And *then* Saint Malo was able to put on his warm hood again.

THE TOWN MOUSE AND THE COUNTRY MOUSE

There were once two mice who were friends. One lived in the town and the other lived in the country.

One day the town mouse went to visit his friend in the country. The country mouse was delighted to see him, and asked him to stay to dinner. He brought out his best food, ears of corn and hips and haws and even a piece of bacon rind which he had stolen from a farm kitchen. But the town mouse did not seem to be enjoying his meal.

'You are not eating very much,' said the country mouse. 'Don't you like my food?'

'I'm sure it's very nice,' said the town mouse. 'But you should just taste the meals I have at home. You really ought to come back to town with me and see how we live there.' And he persuaded his friend to come and pay him a visit in his turn.

When they came to the town, they crept into a fine house which the town mouse said was his home. They went into the dining-room, where the table was covered with scraps left over from a grand party. The town mouse put his country friend on a soft seat and ran about tasting all the good food to find out which were the best bits to put before him. The country mouse ate and ate, and thought that he had never tasted anything so good.

But all at once there was a terrible noise. Doors were being slammed, and a huge dog was barking somewhere. The two mice jumped down from the table in terror and fled into a mouse-hole for safety. They were trembling all over, and half dead with fear.

Then the country mouse said to the town mouse, 'My friend, I am going back home to my quiet little hole in the country. I would much rather have plain food and peace of mind than rich dainties eaten with a fearful heart. Town life is too dangerous for me.'

THE MONK AND THE WOLF

Many years ago there was a monk who lived by himself in the desert. He was a very holy man, who loved God, and the people who came to him for help, and the animals who prowled about in the desert. He was not afraid of them, but treated them as friends and neighbours.

Among the animals there was a wolf who was his special friend. This wolf would come and visit him every day, just at the time he was preparing his dinner of bread and water. He used to share his bread with the wolf; while he ate up his half, the wolf would eat up *his* half, and when he had finished he would lick the man's hand as if to say 'Thank you' and trot off back to the desert.

This went on for many a month, until one day the monk was called away unexpectedly. The wolf arrived as usual at dinner-time, but his friend the monk was nowhere to be seen. He prowled around for a bit, and smelt the bread, and wondered what he ought to do. Should he go away hungry?

Or should he help himself? The bread smelt delicious, and he felt sure the monk would not wish him to go without his dinner. So he knocked the loaf off the table with his paw, gobbled it up and hurried back to his lair, feeling rather uncomfortable.

The monk came back and found the bread gone, and guessed what had happened. But the next day the wolf kept away—he was not at all sure that he wanted to see his friend the monk. He kept away the next day too, and the day after, and the day after that. All this time the monk was wondering what had happened to his friend, and he wished he would come, for he really missed him. But he quite understood that, if the wolf had taken the bread, he might feel awkward about it. But then one day, to the monk's joy, the wolf came trotting up, though not quite so briskly as usual. He came and stood in front of his friend, with his head hanging down in shame.

'You have been a bad wolf,' said the monk, 'but I can see that you are sorry for what you have done. Come and sit down by me, and we will have our dinner together as we used to do.'

So the wolf and the monk were friends again, because the wolf was brave enough to come back and show that he was sorry.

Joan Kendall

THE STORY OF KING MIDAS

Long ago there lived in the land of Greece a king whose name was Midas. He was very, very rich; and he loved being rich. He loved his beautiful palaces, his fine clothes, his dazzling jewels and ornaments. But above all he loved gold itself, the sight of it and the touch of it. He thought it was the most beautiful and desirable thing in the world.

One day he did a kindness to one of the gods—in those days people believed that there were many gods, and that they walked on the earth among men. And as a reward the god, whose name was Dionysius, said that he could have one wish, and it would be granted. What would you have wished for? I expect you would have taken a long time to make up your mind. But Midas said, as quick as a flash, 'Gold! I wish that everything I touch shall turn into gold.'

Dionysius looked rather doubtful, but a promise is a promise, and if that was what King Midas wanted, he must be allowed to have it. So the king set off down the slopes of Mount Olympus, where he had been talking to the god, and when he came to his own lands he began to make experiments. He touched some shiny brown chestnuts, and, sure enough, they turned to gold! The red berries, the trunks of young trees, whole armfuls of branches did the same. He loaded his arms with the stiff gold fruit and leaves, to carry them home; but then he remembered that there was no need—he could make more whenever he liked.

Before very long he arrived home. In an hour he had transformed the palace. He touched everything he could reach, and everything he touched turned to gold—the blue and purple hangings, the scarlet rugs, the soft cushions and comfortable couches, the swords and shields and great wine jars.

All this excitement made him feel hungry, and he looked forward to his dinner with relish. He put on fresh clothes, and as he touched the soft linen of his tunic it turned stiff, and his sandals were difficult to buckle and felt uncommonly hard. However, he avoided touching his girdle until his slaves had tied it up, and it looked very handsome.

King Midas sat down at his table (already pure gold, for he had seen to that), and lifted the wine-glass to his lips. But as the glowing wine touched his mouth, it ceased to flow and became hard and stiff. He lifted a piece of savoury meat to his mouth; it touched his lips, and fell back on his plate with a clang. Panic seized him—was he never going to be able to eat and drink again?

At this moment his little daughter came running in to say good night. Before he could stop her, she had put her arms round his neck, and as she did so she also was turned to gold—a little golden statue. With a cry he lifted it and carried it to her bed. He called to his slaves to keep guard over it, seized his cloak and set off for the mountain to implore the god to undo the terrible wish.

Weeping and stumbling, at last he reached the slopes of Mount Olympus and threw himself at the feet of Dionysius. The god listened gravely to his story, and promised that the power should be taken away. Then the king hurried down the mountainside, and reached his palace as the sun rose. Everything was as he had always known it! How beautiful were the colours of natural things, of flowers and leaves and birds and stones. And in the things he touched there was dryness and wetness, softness and smoothness, crispness and roughness, warmth and coolness; and they remained as they were meant to be. And best of all, his little girl came running towards him, alive and well! Now he could safely catch her in his arms and hug her close; now he could safely sit down to breakfast, for he was very hungry indeed.

I wonder if he told his little girl about what had happened —all because of his own greediness.

Joan Kendall

VI

TIMES AND SEASONS

Spring (Easter)

THE LITTLE YELLOW TULIP

Once there was a little yellow tulip, and she lived down in a little dark house under the ground. One day she was sitting there, all by herself, and it was very quiet. Suddenly she heard a little tap, tap, tap at the door.

'Who is that?' she said.

'It's the rain, and I want to come in,' said a soft, sad little voice.

'No, you can't come in,' the little tulip said.

By and by she heard another little tap, tap, tap on the window-pane.

'Who is there?' she said.

The same soft little voice answered, 'It's the rain, and I want to come in.'

'No, you can't come in,' said the little tulip.

Then it was very quiet for a long time. At last there came a little rustling, whispering sound all round the window: *rustle, whisper, whisper.*

'Who is there?' said the little tulip.

'It's the sunshine,' said a little, soft, cheery voice, 'and I want to come in.'

'N-no,' said the little tulip, 'you can't come in.' And she sat still again.

Pretty soon she heard the little rustling noise at the key-hole.

'Who is there?' she said.

'It's the sunshine,' said the cheery little voice, 'and I want to come in, I want to come in!'

'No, no,' said the little tulip, 'you cannot come in.'

By and by, as she sat so still, she heard tap, tap, tap, and rustle, whisper, rustle up and down the window-pane, and on the door, and at the keyhole.

'Who is there?' she said.

'It's the rain and the sun, the rain and the sun,' said two little voices together, 'and we want to come in. We want to come in. We want to come in!'

'Dear, dear!' said the little tulip, 'If there are two of you, I suppose I shall have to let you in.'

So she opened the door a little wee crack, and in they came. And one took one of her little hands, and the other took her other little hand, and they ran, ran, ran with her, right up to the top of the ground. Then they said, 'Poke your head through!'

So she poked her head through; and she was in the midst of a beautiful garden. It was early springtime, and few other flowers were to be seen; but she had the birds to sing to her and the sun to shine upon her pretty yellow head. She was so pleased, too, when the children cried out with pleasure that now they knew that the beautiful spring had come!

From Stories to Tell to Children *by Sarah Cone Bryant*
(Harrap, 1911).

THE DISOBEDIENT THRUSH

One spring Mr. and Mrs. Thrush made a lovely cosy nest inside a bush in a garden, and Mrs. Thrush laid five pretty pale blue speckled eggs in it. Then she sat on them and kept them warm until they hatched out into five baby thrushes. As soon as the baby thrushes came out of the eggs, they opened their mouths and made loud noises to show that they were hungry and wanted food. Mrs. Thrush gave her babies names because of the noise they made. She called them Eeky, Keeky, Weeky, Squeaky and Squawky. Squawky was the biggest, and he made the loudest noise.

What a din they made, all shouting together! 'Oh dear!' said Father Thrush, 'I shall have to fly round and find them food to eat. You must come with me, my dear,' he said to Mother Thrush. 'I shall never be able to find enough to fill the mouths of so many hungry children.'

'Very well, my dear,' said Mother Thrush, 'I will come with you.' Then she said to the baby thrushes, 'Now, children, I am going out to help your father, and I want you to play quietly in the nest and not fight and squabble. Will you all be very good?' 'Yes, Mummy,' said the five little thrushes; and away their mother flew.

Now Squawky, who was so much bigger than his brothers and sisters, was a very curious little bird, and he wanted to see what it was like outside the nest. So he began to climb up over his brothers and sisters in the nest.

'Ow, that hurts!' said Eeky.

'You shouldn't do that,' said Keeky.

'You're very naughty,' said Weeky.

'You'll fall out,' said Squeaky.

By this time Squawky was standing right on the edge of the nest. 'I shan't fall out,' he said grandly; but he did, you know. He fell right down on the ground under the nest. He was too little to have proper wings to fly with; so down he fell with a big bump, and there he lay on the ground crying loudly.

At first nobody heard him; but presently somebody did. It was a big black pussy cat who had been sitting in the sun. 'Aha!' he said to himself. 'I hear a little bird squawking. I will go and find him. He will do nicely for my tea.' And he came softly padding along.

But then another person heard Squawky crying. He was a boy called John, who lived in the house belonging to the garden. He came out to play, and heard Squawky crying, and went to see what it was, 'Why, you poor little bird!' he said. 'You must have fallen out of your nest. I wonder where it is.'

He looked about to see if he could find it, and there were Mr. and Mrs. Thrush flying round and round, in great trouble. 'Oh dear, oh dear!' Mrs. Thrush was crying. 'Our Squawky has fallen out of the nest, and we can't get him back; and now a huge monster is picking him up, and I'm sure he's going to eat him.' But of course John was not going to eat Squawky. He looked about in the bushes until he found the nest, with the four other baby thrushes in it, and then very gently he put Squawky back in it again beside them. Mrs. Thrush flew down and spread her soft feathers over her babies; and how glad Squawky was, as he cuddled up to her, to find himself safe home again! Mrs. Thrush was so glad to have him back that she didn't scold him; but Squawky said to himself, 'I'm sorry I disobeyed what Mummy told me; I'll never do it again.'

But the black pussy cat had to go somewhere else to find his tea.

BETSY AND THE PANCAKES

A story for Pancake Day—Shrove Tuesday

Once upon a time there was a young woman who lived all alone in a snug little cottage. She liked living alone so that she could think about only herself, about what she could make herself to eat, what she could make herself to wear and what she could do to make her cottage still more cosy and comfy. Her name was Betsy Peabody, but the neighbours called her 'Betsy Meanbody', and indeed she deserved the name, for never had she been known to show the slightest kindness to anyone.

One day Betsy was very happy. It was Pancake Day, and she was making herself a fine feast of pancakes. There she was standing over the fire, frying the pancakes, tossing them in the air, and popping them in the oven to keep nice and hot. 'I'll make myself half a dozen,' she thought, 'and then I'll sit down and eat them all.'

Betsy did as she had planned. Greedily, and all alone, she sat down and ate six great big golden pancakes. And when she had finished them, she sat in her rocking-chair by the fire, thinking of them. Before long, her eyelids began to quiver, her head nodded and she fell fast asleep, and began to dream—of pancakes! There she was, in her dreams, standing over the fire busily frying pancakes, tossing them in the air and popping them into the oven to keep nice and hot. The pile of pancakes grew so enormous that soon they would not fit in the oven at all. 'I'd better start eating them,' thought Betsy. But no sooner had she decided to do this than she heard a timid knock on the door. 'Bother,' she thought, 'who can that be?' And in a very cross voice she called out, 'Come in.'

The door opened slowly and a poor old beggar-woman, leaning on a stick, hobbled in.

'What do you want?' asked Betsy in a voice that would have frightened most people away.

'I was passing your door,' said the old woman, 'and I smelled a good smell of pancakes, and I thought perhaps you might spare me one.'

'Indeed I will not,' answered Betsy. 'These are for me. Now be off with you while I enjoy them.'

'But I have tasted no food since morning. Couldn't you spare me a very small pancake?' pleaded the old woman.

Betsy thought, 'I'll not get rid of her until I give her one. I know what beggars are.' So she said, 'All right, I'll make you just a little one.' And with that she poured a miserable spoonful of batter into the pan. But to her astonishment the batter spread out and rose up into the biggest and most beautiful pancake she had ever seen! The old woman's eyes grew bright with delight as she watched Betsy toss the pancake into the air and catch it again in the clever way she had. 'Oh,' she said, 'what a beautiful pancake! How kind you are!'

'Don't think it is for you,' cried Betsy in such a cross voice that the old woman shrank away from her. 'I said I would make you a little one, didn't I?' And she popped the beautiful big pancake on the top of her own enormous pile.

Then she poured another miserable spoonful of batter into the pan. Again, to her astonishment, the batter spread out and rose into a huge, fluffy pancake. She tossed it in the air and caught it again, and as she did so the old woman clapped her hands delightedly. 'Oh,' she said, 'what a beautiful pancake! How kind you are!'

'Don't think it's for you,' said Betsy, in such a cross voice that the poor old woman trembled with fright. 'I said I'd make you a little one, didn't I? And again she popped the huge, fluffy pancake on the top of her own enormous pile.

Then she again put a miserable spoonful of batter into the pan. Once more the batter spread out and rose up into a tremendous golden pancake. Once more she tossed it in the air and caught it, and once more the old woman clapped her hands.

'Oh,' she said, 'what a beautiful pancake! How kind you are!'

'Don't think . . .' began Betsy; but she never finished what she was saying, for the old woman vanished! She didn't run away or hide herself—quite suddenly she just wasn't there any more! Betsy was frightened. Shaking all over, she staggered to her rocking-chair and sat down. Her hands trembled in her lap, and when she looked at them, she noticed, to her horror, that they were the wrinkled, bony hands of an old woman. She raised them to her face, and when she touched her cheeks she found that they, too, were shrivelled and sunken with age. Betsy groaned aloud, and, then, looking up, she saw a young woman standing over the stove, frying pancakes. Betsy realised what had happened; she had changed places with the old woman. How hungry she was, too! She felt that she would die if she didn't have something to eat quickly.

'Please, could you spare me a pancake?' she asked the young girl, in a voice quivering with weakness.

'Indeed I could not,' answered the young woman in such angry tones that Betsy would have run away had she had strength. 'They are for ME! ME! ME!' The young woman's voice grew louder and louder until Betsy's poor old head was ringing. Betsy shook her head to destroy the noise, and she shook it so hard that she shook herself out of her sleep and her dreams and woke up.

Confused and bewildered, Betsy looked round her. Slowly she realised that it had all been a dream, and that she was still her own young self and nobody else. Betsy was so glad that she wanted to dance and sing and make everybody in the whole world a pancake. She skipped to the door and opened it, and there, in the sunshine outside, she saw some little children playing. 'Come in,' she called to the children 'and I'll make you all pancakes.'

'Pancakes! Pancakes!' shouted the children, running towards Betsy and tumbling over themselves to be the first inside the cottage. 'Sit round the table,' laughed Betsy. 'I'll have the pancakes ready before you can say "Betsy Peabody".' The children needed no second bidding. They arranged themselves round Betsy's table, and clapped and cheered as she tossed the pancakes into the air. And Betsy laughed and laughed as she watched the children gobbling them up, as fast as she could make them. Never in her life had she been so happy; and never had the children enjoyed such a wonderful pancake day.

From A Calendar of Stories *by Lilian McCrea*
(*Sir Isaac Pitman & Sons Ltd., 1957*). *Slightly shortened.*

1. *The Easter-egg hunt*

One Easter holiday Susan went to stay at Willow Tree Farm in the country. At the farm were Susan's Uncle Frank, who was the farmer, and her Auntie May, and her cousin Timothy, who was just about as old as she was. Susan loved staying at the farm, and playing with Timothy. There was such a lot to do. They watched the pig man feeding the pigs, and saw the cows being milked, and helped Auntie May to feed the chickens.

On Easter Saturday Auntie May said to Timothy and Susan, 'I've got a lovely game for you this morning. I have hidden a lot of little Easter eggs for you in the garden. Here is a basket for each of you. Go and see how many you can find.'

So out they went and began to hunt. They went to different parts of the garden to look. And first Susan found a red egg with gold spots in an old flower-pot. Then she found a blue egg in a tuft of grass. And then in an old bird's nest she found two pink eggs with silver patterns on them. Then she went farther up the garden to where there were some bushes. She peeped into one bush, but there were no eggs there. Then she started to peep into another bush—and suddenly there was a most awful noise, cackling and squawking and fluttering, and something came bursting out at her and went screaming and flapping away. Susan was so frightened that she turned and ran away as fast as she could.

But before she ran in to Auntie May, she looked back just to see what it was that had frightened her so badly. And all she saw was a hen walking down the path.

'I wonder—could it have been the hen that made all that noise?' she thought. And she remembered that Auntie May's hens did sometimes make those fluttering and squawking noises. 'I wonder what she was doing in the bush,' she said to herself. So very bravely she tiptoed back to the bush and parted the leaves and looked inside—and there lay four beautiful big brown eggs!

'I've found the most eggs—and the biggest,' she thought; and very carefully she picked them up—they were still warm—and put them in her basket. Then she carried it in to show Auntie May.

'Well,' said Auntie May, 'have you found a nice lot of eggs?'

'Yes,' said Susan. 'Look!' And she held up the basket.

'Wherever did you find those brown eggs?' asked Auntie May.

'Up in a bush in the garden,' said Susan.

'The speckled hen must have laid them,' said Auntie May. 'She always lays brown eggs. I knew she was getting out to lay her eggs, but I couldn't find the nest. I *am* pleased that you have found it, Susan. Now you and Timothy can each have a brown egg for your breakfast on Easter morning.'

Just then Timothy came in with his basket. 'I found more eggs than you, Susan,' said he.

'Yes—but mine were real ones,' said Susan.

2. New things at Easter-time

Susan was having a lovely time on her holiday at Willow Tree Farm, with her Uncle Frank, the farmer, and her Auntie May and her cousin Timothy, who was just about as old as she was.

There were such lots of interesting things to do at the farm. Especially Susan loved looking at the baby animals. There were so many of them. In the sty lay the old mother pig, with all her baby piglets squealing and scuffling round her. Out in the field were the sheep, and they had baby lambs skipping and running everywhere. The mother horse in the paddock had a beautiful little foal. And Auntie May took Susan into the cowshed to see the baby calf which had just been born to Daisy the cow.

'What a lot of little new things there are,' she said to Auntie May.

'Yes,' said Auntie May. 'New things come at Easter-time.'

Then one day Susan was playing in the big dark barn, and in a corner she saw what looked like a little house. It had a sack thrown over it, and Susan was just going to lift up the sack to see what was underneath it when there came such a funny squawking noise that she was frightened and ran away and told Auntie May.

'Oh, that's my old hen Biddy,' said Auntie May. 'She likes to be shut up in the hen coop in the dark when she is sitting on some eggs.'

'Why is she sitting on them?' asked Susan.

'To keep them warm,' said Auntie May. 'Inside each egg there is a baby chick, and if Biddy sits on the eggs and keeps them warm for a long, long time, then one day there will be a tapping noise inside one of the eggs, and the egg shell will crack, and out will come a baby chick. Then all the eggs will crack, and soon Biddy will have a new family. I think the eggs will start cracking very soon now.'

Sure enough, one morning when Auntie May came in to wake Susan up, she said, 'Dress quickly, Susan, and run down to the lawn in front of the house. There's something there for you to see.' So Susan got dressed and ran downstairs, and there on the lawn was the little house, the hen coop, but there was no sack over it now. And in front of it was what looked like a long box made of wire, so that you could see inside it.

Susan stooped down to talk to Biddy in the coop. 'Hullo, Biddy,' she said. And then she cried, 'Oh! Oh!' because something was peeping out from under the mother hen's wing. It was a little yellow head. And there was another— and another. And then a little yellow chick ran out into the wire pen on the grass. He was followed by a little brother or sister, and soon there were a whole lot of little yellow chicks running about and calling 'Cheep! Cheep!'

'Perhaps they are hungry,' thought Susan. And just then she heard Auntie May's voice. 'Here you are, little ones,' she said; and she opened up the wire pen and put in a saucer of food.

'Now, Susan, you come and have your breakfast too,' she said, 'and then you can come out and watch the chicks again.'

How Susan loved those chicks! She was always watching them. She specially liked to see them run to their mother when she called, and hide away under her wings, with their little heads just peeping out.

Susan was really sorry when the day came for her to go home again.

'Oh, I don't want to leave the chicks,' she said. 'I wish I could take them with me.'

'Don't you want to see your mummy again?' said Auntie May.

'Oh yes, of course,' said Susan.

'And I think she may have something special for you at home,' said her aunt.

'Oh, what? What?' Susan cried; but her auntie wouldn't say.

'It's a surprise,' was all she said.

So Auntie May took Susan home; and when they got there, she said, 'Run up and see Mummy. She's in her room.'

So Susan ran upstairs, and there was her mummy in bed. Susan climbed on to the bed, and they hugged and hugged. Then Susan said, 'Auntie May says you've got something nice to show me.'

'Yes,' said her mummy. 'There it is.' And she showed Susan a little cot by the bed. In the cot was what Susan at first thought was a dolly. But it opened its mouth and yawned, and then she saw that it was a real baby.

'Oh! Oh!' said Susan, just as she did when she saw the baby chicks.

'It's a new baby brother for you,' said her mummy.

'Oh, is he really mine?' cried Susan. 'My very own brother? How lovely! You told me a new baby was coming, but I didn't know it would be so soon.' She didn't mind now about leaving the chicks behind. She ran to Auntie May.

'Oh, Auntie, Auntie,' she cried. 'Mummy's hatched out a baby brother for me.'

'I told you that new things come at Easter-time,' said Auntie May.

Summer Holidays

BRAVE BILLY

Billy was five, and his little sister Mary was three; and they were going for a holiday at the seaside with their daddy and mummy.

When they got to the seaside, Billy and Mary and their daddy and mummy went down to the beach. Billy thought it was a lovely place. It was a sunny day; the sand was white and the sea was blue. Billy and Mary had a fine time chasing each other over the sand. Then they put on their bathing things and went down to the sea.

Billy and Mary had never seen the sea before. Mary loved it, and she let her daddy carry her right into the water and jump up and down with her. But Billy didn't like it. He had never seen so much water before; and the water was very cold, and it didn't stay still—it kept coming up to him as if it were trying to catch him. He was really frightened, and he ran away. So Mummy and Daddy and Mary had a happy time splashing in the water, but though they called to Billy, he wouldn't come in with them. He went off on his own.

Presently he found a little pool, which was not very deep and had interesting things in it, and he played in that till Mummy called him to dinner. After dinner Mary went back to play in the sea, and Daddy and Mummy lay down for a nap, and Billy began to make a sand castle with his spade.

He made a fine big castle, and then he climbed up on top of it and called out, 'Look at me!' But he couldn't see his daddy and mummy. They had gone to talk to some people farther along the beach. And when he looked at Mary— what do you think she was doing? She had found a little rubber boat which someone had left, and she was sitting in it playing with some stones.

Billy went on building his castle. When he looked up again, Mary was still sitting in the boat. But Billy saw that the boat was floating in the water, and the waves were washing it away from the shore. Every moment it was going farther and farther out into deep water.

'Daddy! Daddy!' shouted Billy. 'Come quick!' And he ran into the water just a little way. It was cold, but he didn't mind—he was thinking so much about Mary. Then Daddy came rushing along and waded into the sea and caught hold of the little rubber boat and began to pull it back to land. Billy helped him; and now there was Mummy coming out into the water too. She picked up Mary and hugged her, while Daddy and Billy brought the little boat right up on to the shore.

'Good for you, Billy!' said Daddy. 'It was lucky you were watching, or Mary might have gone right out to sea. And you were brave to come into the water to help me when you are afraid of the sea.'

But Billy said, 'I wasn't afraid, Daddy—not one little bit.'

And do you know, he was never frightened of the sea again. He and Mary went in to bathe every day of their holiday, and they played wonderful splashing games in the water, and altogether it was a lovely holiday.

PRUNELLA THE PEBBLE

There was once a plain little pebble on a large beach. Her name was Prunella. Other pebbles on the beach were brown, black or white; but Prunella was just a dull grey. On sunny days in summer, mothers, fathers, aunts, uncles, sons, daughters and cousins used to come to the beach and sit in the sun, bathe in the sea or go for walks along the shore; they would usually look at the pebbles on the beach and say how pretty were the brown, black or white pebbles, but no one talked about Prunella the grey pebble. This made Prunella very sad. She was not a proud pebble, but like everyone else, she liked to be noticed once in a while.

Then one night, when all the other pebbles were asleep, and Prunella lay thinking, a beautiful seagull landed on a rock near her. 'Don't worry,' said the seagull. 'I have seen this happen before. You will be needed some time.'

The next day was very cloudy and windy, and few people came on the beach. The tide came and tossed and pushed the other pebbles; but Prunella was left where she was. The tide came very near, but it turned back before it reached her. Then there was a storm. The rain came down, and there was thunder and lightning. Then Prunella suddenly saw a little fishing boat out on the sea. It had been caught in the storm, and it was trying to reach the shore. She watched it as it came nearer and nearer, till at last the fishermen in it were able to land it safely on the beach. They were very thankful to be safe. They got out and sheltered by a large rock. They had brought a little stove with them, and some coffee which they tried to heat on the stove. But the wind kept blowing the stove over, and it would not stay steady. The fishermen built a little wall round it made of pebbles, but still it would not stay steady. Then one of the fishermen said, 'Ah!', and picked up Prunella. 'This pebble will do it,' he said. 'Just the right size and shape.' And he cleverly slipped Prunella into a hole in the little wall where she just fitted in nicely. At last the stove stood steady, and the coffee began to get hot. The wall protected the flame, and soon the fishermen were drinking good hot coffee and feeling much better.

The storm ended, and the fishermen sailed away their

boat. And Prunella was left behind feeling very proud that she had been useful. It was just as the seagull had said—she had been needed.

Juliet Brittain

TUGGY AND THE BIG SHIP

Tuggy was a happy little tug-boat who lived in one of the great ports of Britain. He was happy because he was able to help the big ships come in and out of port. When they came in from the sea, he would tie himself up to them and pull them until they were safely along the quayside. Then, while he watched their cargoes being unloaded, the ships would tell him about their exciting adventures all over the world.

But in the port was a big ship called Murdoch, who had no use for the other ships, and especially not for tugs. Some of the tugs were angry with Murdoch, some were afraid, and others went off to another part of the dock to get away from this bad-tempered big ship.

Tuggy saw what was happening. He wasn't angry, and he wouldn't go to another part of the dock. He wasn't afraid either; but he did think that Murdoch could be more polite and friendly to the other ships.

One day Murdoch came back from a voyage and thought that he would move into port by himself, without a tug to help him. All the ships watched breathlessly as he slowly steamed into the dock and came alongside the quay. Murdoch was very happy to have done it all by himself. But all the other ships were gloomy. The tugs were especially worried. 'If the big ships can come in by themselves like that,' they said to each other, 'they won't need us any longer.' The ships said nasty things about Murdoch; but Tuggy did not say anything.

Weeks passed, and at last Murdoch was due back from another voyage. There was a great storm, with thunder and lightning, rain, a strong wind and high waves like mountains. All the ships and tugs hurried into port, and tied up at the quayside where they were safe. But not Tuggy—he was thinking about Murdoch. The other tugs laughed at him. 'If Murdoch wants to move into port without a tug in fine weather, then he can do it in a storm as well,' they said.

But Tuggy waited outside the entrance of the port, in the cold, the thunder, the rain, the wind and the high seas. Big waves washed over his deck, and he was very cold. At last, when Tuggy was very tired from battling against the sea, he saw a ship come steaming slowly towards him. It was Murdoch. Murdoch told Tuggy that only one of his engines was working, and he said he would be glad if Tuggy would tow him into port. So in they came, the little tug-boat first and the great big ship coming slowly after him. All the ships were watching. As soon as Murdoch was safely tied alongside the quay, he spoke out so that all the other ships could hear.

'I want to thank Tuggy,' he said, 'for bringing me in safely. I thought I could manage without little ships; but now I know that I can't. Where would we big ships be in storms like this one if it wasn't for the little ships?'

Then all the big ships blew their sirens, and all the little ships cheered and had lumps in their throats. But Tuggy just chuckled and went happily back to his berth.

Juliet Brittain

Autumn (Harvest)

TWO EARS OF CORN

One day a farmer said, 'I am going to sow some corn.' So he ploughed the ground, and made it all smooth and soft, and then he planted the corn in it.

'Isn't this a lovely soft bed?' said one little seed of corn.

'Yes, it is,' said his friend who lay beside him. 'We shall

grow well here.' And they began to grow and grow. They put out little roots, and sucked up the good water in the ground, and when the rain came falling, pit-a-patter, they sucked up that too. 'It's good,' said the two little seeds of corn. And they grew and grew.

Then the sun came out, and he shone down on the field. He made the two little seeds feel all warm and cosy. 'It's good,' said the two little seeds of corn. And they grew and grew.

They grew till they were tall stalks, each with a big ear of corn on the top of it, filled with tiny seeds. 'We are fine fellows now,' said the two seeds of corn. And still they grew and grew.

Then one day the farmer came into the field. He saw the two fine ears of corn, standing there so ripe and yellow, and he felt them with his hands, and looked at all the other ears, and said, 'Tomorrow this field shall be reaped.'

The next day there was a great banging and rattling in the field, and all the ears of corn were cut and bundled together and stacked. Then they were put into a threshing machine, which rattled and banged till all the chaff was gone. Then they were ground up into flour, and they didn't like that very much. But at last it was done, and they were put into sacks to go to the baker's.

'How are you feeling?' said one ear of corn to the other.

'Fine,' said his friend. 'I wonder what comes next.'

What came next was that they were made into bread and put in an oven.

'How are you feeling now?' said one little ear of corn to the other.

'Fine,' said the other little ear of corn, 'but rather hot.'

At last the bread was ready and put in the shop to be sold. And a lady came and bought the loaf that had the two little friends in it and took it home for her little boy and girl to eat. She buttered two slices for them when they came in for their tea. The little girl was hungry, and ate up all her slice; but the little boy only bit one mouthful out of his piece, and put it down.

'Eat up your bread and butter, darling,' said his mother.

'Don't want it,' said the little boy. And he went out to play. But after a time he felt hungry, and came indoors.

'Can I have my bread and butter now?' he asked.

'Yes, you can,' said his mother. 'It is a good thing you came in, because I was going to throw it in the dustbin. And that would have been a waste.'

It would have been a waste, wouldn't it? Think of all the work the farmer did, and the rain, and the sun, and the baker, and the shopman *and* the two little ears of corn—it was a good thing the little boy ate his bread and butter all up.

WHAT HAPPENED TO THE HARVEST MICE

Mother and Father Harvest Mouse had built their home in a cornfield. It was a nest shaped like a ball, hanging between five corn stalks. There was a family in the nest, six naked babies that squirmed and wriggled and hadn't yet opened their eyes. Mother Harvest Mouse fed them patiently, making little trips from time to time in search of food for herself. Father Harvest Mouse, though not much use with the babies, was usually not far away.

'I think,' said Mother Harvest Mouse one morning, 'I think I fancy a nice grain of corn.' So she left her babies to sleep and, shutting the door very carefully behind her, climbed up one of the corn stalks to find what she wanted.

A lark was singing and circling in the sky when, suddenly, he dropped and came to rest close to Mother Harvest Mouse where she sat nibbling an ear of corn.

'My dear,' twittered the lark, 'such a commotion, do you hear? The men have come to start the harvesting.'

'No, I hadn't heard,' said Mrs. Harvest Mouse, placidly munching.

'But what will you *do*?' cried the lark. 'My family fortu-

nately flew this morning, so I will take them over the wall
to the hillside. You had better do the same.'

'No,' said Mother Harvest Mouse. 'My family can't fly.
I won't do that.'

'Well, don't say I didn't warn you,' said Lark, flying off
to collect the baby larks.

Mother Harvest Mouse finished her meal and went back
to the nest. Father Mouse had heard the news too, and met
her on the way.

'Shall we build a new nest across the wall,' he suggested,
'and carry the babies there?'

'No,' said Mother Harvest Mouse, as she went into the
nest to feed her babies; 'there's no time. We won't do that.'

The whirr of the harvester and the shouts of the men could
be heard when Mother Harvest Mouse went for her next
meal. She fancied a morsel of groundsel this time, so she
slid down a corn stalk to the ground. Rabbit came up as she
nibbled at the groundsel leaf.

'Do you hear?' cried Rabbit in a flutter. 'They've started
harvesting. I'm just going to fetch my family. We shall go
over the wall and find a new home on the hillside. You had
better do the same.'

Mother Harvest Mouse sneezed as a groundsel head blew
away, tickling her nose with its feathery tufts as it passed.
'No,' said Mother Harvest Mouse. 'Atishoo! It is too far.
No; I won't do that.'

'Well, don't say I didn't warn you,' said Rabbit, hurrying
away to fetch her family. Mother Harvest Mouse watched
her go. Then she went back to her babies.

Next, Dormouse hurried by, carrying one of her babies.
'The harvesters are coming,' she said. 'I'm taking my babies
to shelter in the wall. This is the last one. You had better do
the same.'

'No,' said Mother Harvest Mouse. 'My babies are all too
young. I shan't do that.'

After Dormouse came Hare, followed by two skipping

babies, and after Hare, Mice and Voles, all with their families. They each told Mother Harvest Mouse what they were going to do, and suggested that she should do the same, but she said 'No' to all of them, while the sound of the harvester came nearer.

Hedgehog came last with four pale little hedgehog youngsters close behind. 'They are nearly here,' said Hedgehog. 'We are going over the wall to hide under the bracken. You had better come with us.'

'No,' said Mother Harvest Mouse. 'My babies might get lost in the bracken. I shan't do that.'

Mother Harvest Mouse watched the hedgehogs till they were out of sight, and she listened to the sound of the harvester as it came nearer. Then suddenly she became very busy. She scurried all over their nest, pushing here and pulling there. Then she hurried inside and shut the door. The noise of the harvester came nearer—nearer—very near— the nest quivered and shook and began to fall.

'Hold tight, everyone,' said Mother Harvest Mouse as they went down. They didn't go far, and there was only a little bump at the bottom. But that was not all. After the bump it was quiet for a time, then the whole nest was tossed and turned this way and that way, till it was a good thing that mice don't mind very much which way up they are, and that the nest, being round, didn't matter at all. Then came another long pause, followed by more tossings and turnings and bumpings and a rather squashed feeling— finally, one last bump. And then all was quiet.

'Well!' said Mother Harvest Mouse presently, and started to feed her babies. When the babies were fed, Mother Harvest Mouse said she was hungry, so very carefully she peeped out of the front door. . . .

Everything was different! No blue or grey sky stretched overhead, no waving corn stalks all around. Instead, the dark beams of an old barn were above, and neat bundles of cut corn were piled up to the roof.

'That's all right,' she said contentedly—and indeed it was. They were warm and dry (in the barn) and sheltered from the winter weather that must soon be coming, and with more food than an army of mice would need.

'What more could we want?' said Mother Harvest Mouse. And what more could they?

From Stories of an Old Grey Wall *by Cicely Englefield (Evans Bros. Ltd., 1962). Very slightly adapted.*

A HARVEST STORY

This is a story about how the world was troubled and sad after the harvest had been taken from her, and how she was comforted.

The apple trees were the first to speak. They said, 'All our fruit has been taken away. During the spring and during the summer we put all our strength into making big rosy apples. Now the men have put their ladders against our branches, and picked our fruit and taken it from us. What shall we do without our fruit? Soon our leaves will drop off and blow away, and our branches will be bare, and we shall be cold. What shall we do when the winter comes?'

Then another voice spoke up. It was a hard, dry, rattly voice, and it came from a green poppy head. The poppy head said, 'What shall I do when the winter comes? In the summer I had shining red petals as soft as silk, and everyone stopped to say how beautiful I was. Before long even my strong stem will rot, and there will be nothing left of me!'

Then the fields spoke. 'Oh dear,' they said, 'we are feeling so cold and bare. In the spring we were covered with a hundred thousand bright green shoots. They grew to the height of a child, and turned from green, first to pale gold, and then to a deep burnt gold. The farmers used to walk along our paths and rub the ears of corn between their hands and say, "It will be a good harvest." But now they have shaved us clean, and all that is left is the hard prickly stubble. What shall we do when the winter comes?'

Then other voices piped up—the voices of rabbits. 'It is worse for us,' they said. 'We always used to play in the corn-fields. No one could see us and no one could catch us, and we had fine fun.'

'But it is even worse for us,' said the little field mice, 'be-cause we used to *live* in the cornfields. That's where we made our home. And now our homes are bare and open, and we have nowhere to go for the winter.'

Then God, who created all living things, apples and corn, and poppies and rabbits and mice, as well as men and women, heard this sad cry coming up from the earth, and He sent an angel to comfort them all. First the angel flew to the apple trees, and said to them, 'Surely you have not forgotten? It was the same last autumn, and the autumn before, and every other autumn since the world began. Your fruit must go to feed the children of men, for that is why you were created. But at every place where one of your leaves falls, a little hard brown bud is left, and in the bud, packed very small and tight, is a new leaf and a new flower and a new apple. Wait patiently, for God has promised that the spring will come.'

Then the angel flew to the poppy. Now the poppy had only been alive for a few months, and could not be expected to remember. So the angel said to the poppy, 'You have no need to be sad. In your head are a hundred black seeds. Shake your head, and they will be scattered over the earth; and when the spring comes, instead of one red poppy, there will be a hundred. You must believe me when I tell you this, for it has always been so. Wait patiently, for God has promised that the spring will come.'

Then the angel flew to the cornfields, and said to them, 'Surely *you* haven't forgotten? There are bad times coming, for your earth will be cut and turned by the plough, and you will be covered by a blanket of snow. But wait patiently, for new corn will be sown, and God has promised that the spring will come.'

Next, the angel spoke to the rabbits and the field mice, and said, 'Even though the corn is cut, you have other homes for the winter. The days will grow shorter and the nights will grow longer, but winter is a warm and cosy time for those who have burrows and nests. And if you wait patiently the spring will come, for God has promised that it shall be so.'

So, when the angel had comforted the earth, he flew back to God, and the earth settled down to wait patiently, for they knew that another spring would not be very long before it came.

Joan Kendall
Church of England Newspaper, 1960

Winter (Christmas)

THE LEGEND OF THE EVERGREENS

You know that there are some trees, like the holly and the laurel, whose leaves do not fall off in the winter. This is a story about them.

Once upon a time there was a poor little bird who had broken one of his wings. He lived in a country where the winters were very cold; so all his family and playfellows flew away to a warmer country when the days grew shorter. But he could not fly because of his broken wing.

'What shall I do?' he said to himself, when all his companions had gone and the winds blew strong and cold. 'I will creep into the forest and try to keep warm.' So he fluttered and hopped along until he came to a beautiful elm tree.

'Tall and stately elm,' he said, 'will you let me live in your branches and keep me warm while the cold weather lasts?'

'No,' said the elm. 'You will be in my way. I shall not be able to rustle my leaves nicely with a silly little bird in my branches.'

So the poor little bird was turned shivering away. After fluttering about a little, he saw an oak tree, and went to him with the same plea.

'Get away!' said the oak. 'I won't have you here. I know you—you want to eat my acorns.'

Again the little bird went sadly away. Then he saw the beautiful silver birch. She looked so pretty in her gown of silver and green that he hopped up to her, hoping that she would have pity on him. But no. She looked down disdainfully at the poor little bird and said, 'Go away; I do not care to talk to strangers.'

So the poor little bird sat sadly down under a spruce tree. 'I shall die,' he said, 'for no one will have anything to do with me.'

'Don't say that,' said the kind-hearted spruce. 'You may have a home in my branches, and I will try to keep you warm.'

A handsome pine tree was standing near. 'I will keep the wind off you,' he said. 'You may hop about in the soft carpet under my trunk whenever you like.'

'And you can come and eat my berries whenever you are hungry,' said a jolly old holly tree.

'When it is very windy you may come to me,' said the cedar. 'I have lovely tents under my branches.'

'When you feel better you may come and play with my tassels,' said the larch.

'When it snows you may come and hide under me,' said the laurel bush. 'My leaves are thick and waterproof.'

The fairy of the fields and forests, who looks after all the trees and flowers, had heard all that had been going on, and that evening she went on a visit to the Frost King.

'I have put my flowers to bed for the winter, your Majesty,' she said, 'and all the trees are ready to have their old clothes stripped off them. So we are ready for you whenever you like to come.'

Then she told him the tale of the little bird, and said, 'Will it please your Majesty not to touch the trees that have been so kind to him? Will you allow them to keep their leaves?

So the mighty Frost King went silently through the woods that cold moonlight night, and in the morning nearly all the trees had lost their leaves. But the spruce, the pine, the holly, the cedar, the larch and the laurel bush were as green as ever. And that is how they became evergreens.

> *From* A Sheaf of Stories *by Theodora Horton*
> (*National Christian Education Committee*).

THE SNOW-MAN

Martin and Terry woke up one Saturday morning. They looked round their room. It seemed different somehow from the way it looked yesterday. Then Martin jumped out of bed and ran to the window.

'Oh, Terry, come and look!' he cried. 'It's snow!'

Terry jumped out too and rushed to the window. The ground outside was all white with deep snow. The milkman was just coming up the path with the milk, but you couldn't hear his footsteps because the snow was so soft and deep.

Just then the boys' mother came in. They both rushed to her. 'Mummy, Mummy, snow!' they shouted. 'Can we go out in it?'

'Breakfast first,' she said. In no time they were dressed and hurrying downstairs, eager to be out of doors in the snow.

'You must eat a good breakfast,' their mother said. 'That will keep you warm when you are playing outside.' So they ate it all up, every bit, and then she wrapped them up in warm clothes, with their wellingtons and their gloves, and out they went into the snow.

'I'll come out presently,' their daddy called as they went out, 'as soon as I've finished the job I'm doing.'

What fun they had in the snow! They kicked it up with their boots, and threw snowballs at each other, and shouted and laughed.

Presently Martin said, 'I'm going to make a snow-man.'

'Can I help?' asked Terry.

'No, you can't,' said Martin. 'It's going to be my very own snow-man, and I'm going to make it all by myself.'

Terry was very sad. He did so want to make a snow-man. He tried to make one of his own, but he didn't know how. He threw snowballs at the tree-trunks, and shook the snow off the bushes; but he felt very cross. And he got crosser and crosser.

Presently the boys' mother called, 'Come in now, boys; I've got some lovely hot cocoa ready to warm you up.'

'Yum! Yum!' said Martin, and he went rushing indoors. Terry went in slowly, because he was still feeling cross. He passed by Martin's snow-man and stopped to look at it. And then he did a very dreadful thing. He kicked that snow-man all to pieces!

He didn't feel at all nice inside after he had done it. But he went indoors and drank his cocoa, and then he and Martin went out again. But when Martin saw his snow-man all spoilt, he said, 'Terry! You've knocked down my snow-man!' He was furious.

'Well, you wouldn't let me help you,' said Terry. He was furious too. They began to shout and punch each other, and they made so much noise that their daddy came out to see what was going on.

'Hullo—what's the matter?' he asked. Martin and Terry both started to tell him. 'He spoilt my snow-man.' 'He wouldn't let me help him.'

'I'll tell you what we'll do,' said the boys' father. 'We'll all three build a big snow-man together. How about that?'

'Oh yes, yes!' cried the boys, forgetting all about their

quarrel; and they gathered up the bits of Martin's old snow-man, and added lots and lots more snow. The snow-man grew and grew. First he was taller than Terry; then he was taller than Martin; and at last he was very nearly as tall as Daddy.

'There,' said Daddy, 'I think that's big enough. Now we must dress him.' So he fetched one of his own old hats and put it on the snow-man's head, and made him a face, and Terry found two stones for his eyes, and Martin found some shiny bottle-tops to make his buttons, and Daddy gave him a piece of wood as a pipe, and then he was all ready.

'Come and see, Mummy,' they called. 'Come and see our snow-man.'

So out came Mummy, and she brought a piece of red woollen stuff to make the snow-man a cosy scarf.

'He's beautiful,' she said. 'What a good job you've done! Now come on in—dinner's ready.'

'It's more fun working together than working by one-self, isn't it, Martin?' said Daddy, as they walked up the path.

'Yes, it is,' said Martin. And he felt sorry he had not wanted Terry to help before.

'That's right,' said Terry. 'And making things is more fun than breaking things.'

And then they all went in to dinner.

THE MOTHER WHO WAS WAITING FOR HER BABY

The Christmas story

Once there was a mother who was waiting for her Baby to be born. She had everything ready for Him—His little clothes and His little bed. 'Soon He will come,' she thought, 'and I will wrap Him in these little clothes, and lay Him in this little bed, and sing Him to sleep, and we will be so happy.'

But one day her husband Joseph came to her and said,

'Wife, we have to go on a journey. I must go to the town of Bethlehem, and I cannot leave you here alone, so you must come with me.'

'Oh,' cried the mother, 'but what about my Baby when He comes? What about His little clothes and His little bed?'

'You can take the clothes with you,' said Joseph. 'And we must find a bed for Him when we get there.'

'Very well,' said the mother. So she packed the little clothes, and Joseph brought his donkey, and she sat on it, and away they went—clip-clop, clip-clop—on a long, long journey.

When they came to the town of Bethlehem, the mother was very tired. 'Oh, I do want to find a bed for my Baby!' she said. 'Perhaps He will be born tonight. Please, Joseph, knock on somebody's door and ask.'

So Joseph went to a door and knocked. 'Can I bring in a mother who is waiting for her Baby?' he asked. But the people inside said, 'No room, no room!' So the little donkey had to go clip-clopping along once more.

Presently they came to another place. 'Ask again,' said the mother. So Joseph asked; but the people inside said, 'No room, no room!' So the little donkey had to go clip-clopping along once more.

They tried and tried, but everyone said, 'No room, no room!' But at last a man said, 'I have no room, but there is room in the stable, where the cows and other animals are.'

'That will do,' said Joseph. So the man took them into his stable, and the little donkey went in, clip-clop, clip-clop; and when they were inside, the mother said, 'Oh, look! There is the place where they put the hay for the cows and horses to eat—the manger. It has nice soft hay in it. That will make a little bed for my Baby.'

So that night the mother's little Baby was born. And she wrapped Him in the little clothes, and laid Him in His manger bed, and sang Him to sleep, just as she had planned, and they were all so happy. And the mother's name was

Mary, and the Baby's name was Baby Jesus. Had you guessed that already?

THE ANGEL WHO WAS ALWAYS LATE

Once there was a little angel who was always late. He was never there when he ought to be. He had things to do, like all angels; but if he was doing something he liked, he went on doing it long after he should have been doing something else. And if it was something he didn't like, it was just the same; he took so long to begin it that he was never finished in time for the next thing. And sometimes he didn't do anything at all—he just sat on a cloud and dreamed.

One day he was doing that—just sitting on a cloud—when a lot of little angels came hurrying past. 'Come on, slowcoach!' they shouted. 'The archangels want us.' The archangels are the big angels who tell the little angels what to do.

So the little angel who was always late went with the other little angels, and they found all the angels in heaven crowded together in the sky. And one of the archangels, with beautiful coloured wings. was talking to them.

'Today is a very important day,' he was saying. 'If you look down to earth, you can see a little town called Bethlehem. Tonight in that little town there is going to be born the most wonderful Baby in the world, and we are going to sing a song for Him. So you must all be in your places.'

'How shall we know when it is time to sing?' asked an angel.

'Do you see that big bright star in the sky?' said the archangel. 'It is a new star, and it is coming towards us. As soon as you see that star right over Bethlehem, then is the time to sing.'

The angels all went off to do the things they had to do, and the angel who was always late went back to his cloud, and thought about all the things he had heard—the beautiful new star, and the wonderful Baby, and the song the angels were going to sing; and he forgot all about everything. He just sat there, until suddenly he looked up at the new star, and saw that it was nearly over Bethlehem.

'Oh dear, I must hurry,' he thought. 'I mustn't be late for the singing.' But all this time thick clouds had been coming up, and he couldn't see his way through them. He tried to push them aside, but he didn't know which way to go. 'I must ask help from my loving heavenly Father,' he thought; so he prayed a little prayer. 'Dear Father God,' he said, 'I'm sorry I was late. Please show me the way to go.'

At once the clouds cleared away, and there were all the angels, shining row upon row. The archangel was just saying, 'Where is the little angel who sings in the top right-hand corner?' when that very same little angel came bursting out of the clouds and scuttled into his place just in time. For at that moment all the heavenly host burst into their wonderful song: and this is what they sang:

> Glory to God in the highest,
> And on earth peace,
> Good will towards men.

And whenever you hear that song at Christmas, remember the little angel who was always late. But he wasn't late that time, was he?

TWO LITTLE ANGELS AT CHRISTMAS

Two little angels were sitting on a cloud when they saw a lot of other angels hurrying past them.

'Where are you going?' they called out.

'To see the wonderful Baby who has just been born,' they called back.

'Wait for us,' the little angels cried. 'Where is the Baby?'

'You will find Him where the star stops,' cried the angels; and they hurried on. The two little angels went after them as quickly as they could; but they were very small, and could not go very fast, and the bigger angels were soon out of sight.

The little angels went on and on; and presently they came to a big palace.

'The wonderful Baby will surely be in that palace,' they said; so in they went and looked round. They looked in the great hall, where the king was having his grand dinner; they looked in all the rooms; they even looked in the kitchen where the grand dinner was cooked. But there was no Baby there; so they went on again.

Presently they came to a temple, a place like a big church. 'The wonderful Baby will surely be in that temple,' they said; so in they went and looked round. There were people inside holding a service; and they looked round everywhere, among the people who were singing and the people who were praying. But there was no Baby there; so they went on again.

Presently they came to a house called an inn, where people came to have a meal and sleep for the night.

'Perhaps the wonderful Baby will be here,' said one little angel.

'Yes,' said the other little angel. 'Look! The big star is right over it, just as the angels said. This must be the place.' So in they went and looked around. There were people eating and drinking, and talking and laughing; but there was no Baby there. So out they came again.

'There isn't anywhere else to look,' said one little angel. 'We had better go back. But I don't understand about the star—the angels said the Baby would be in the place where it stopped, and this is the place.'

'No, it isn't,' said the other little angel. 'Look! The star is not above the inn, it is above that little building like a shed at the side of the inn. The Baby must be there.'

'In that poor little shed?' said the other little angel. 'Oh, surely not.'

'Let us go and look,' said the first little angel; so in they went. And there were all the other angels crowded round a cattle stall, and there was the Baby lying in the manger, and there was His mother looking at Him so proudly and lovingly; and there was a kind-looking man standing by them, and oxen and donkeys looking on. And then the two little angels knew that they had found what they were looking for; and they were very, very glad that Christmas night.

THE PAPER ANGEL

The little paper angel swung round and round on the Christmas tree. To look at, he was just like any other paper angel. Sally had made him only yesterday. He had two white wings, and a full white skirt, and two white arms sticking out in which he held a carol book. He had a piece of red silk thread stuck on to the back of his head, from which he swung on the Christmas tree. But really the paper angel was quite different from any other paper angel. Behind his paper arms and carol book he had a heart. And he had a heart because Sally, who made him, had put a whole lot of love into making him. So the paper angel felt things and thought things as he danced at the end of his bit of red silk.

Most of all he was thinking about Sally. Sally had gone to bed feeling very cross that evening. Her baby brother Michael had broken her best little blue china teapot; and though Mother had said she would mend it, Sally had been very cross with Michael.

'He shan't *ever* play with *any* of my toys *ever* again!' she had said. 'He always breaks things.' And Michael had cried. But Sally hadn't been sorry one little bit.

A little wind came in at the open window, and the paper angel swung round and round and round, faster than ever. Suddenly he swung right off the Christmas tree in the corner into the middle of the room, his wings fluttering a little and his heart fluttering a lot. Away out of the door he fluttered, across the landing, and right into the room where Sally and Michael were lying asleep in their two beds. The paper angel didn't stop until he reached Sally's pillow, and there he rested on his funny round skirt.

Sally was fast asleep and dreaming. In her dream she was saying, 'SHAN'T! SHAN'T! SHAN'T!' And the paper angel, because he had a heart himself, could see right inside Sally's heart. He was very sad when he saw the naughty thoughts there, because he liked Sally. She was a very nice little girl most of the time, and had a very loving heart. But just at this minute Sally loved the little blue teapot more than she loved her little brother Michael.

So the paper angel thought and thought, and suddenly he said to himself: 'I'll go to the place where all the happy thoughts come from, and I'll bring one back for Sally.' So he called to the little wind, and the wind came and picked him up and carried him out of the window, and away, away up in the air, to the place where all the happy thoughts come from.

It was cold and dark on the earth that night; but away up in the sky all was warm and bright and beautiful. In the middle of the place where all the happy thoughts come from was a tree lit up. It was like a big, big Christmas tree. Real stars hung on its branches, and there was a real angel standing on the very top. Hanging on the tree were hundreds and hundreds of little coloured parcels, tied up with gay pieces of silk and ribbon.

The paper angel went round and round, peeking at them all. Now and again he looked at a label. At last he found a little parcel wrapped in pale pink paper with green leaves and holly berries painted all over it. It was tied with green ribbon, and on the label was written the little word, 'SHARE'.

Then the paper angel asked the angel on the top of the tree, very politely, if he could take away that parcel and give it to Sally. And the angel said yes, he could. So down through the air the wind carried the paper angel and the parcel, right back to Sally's home, and in through the window to the pillow of Sally's bed. The paper angel put down his gay little parcel, unbuttoned Sally's heart, took out the untidy, grubby little parcel inside which had 'SHAN'T!' written all over it, and was simply bulging with all the naughty things bursting out of it. In its place he popped the little parcel labelled 'SHARE'.

The wind blew the grubby little parcel out of the window and right away, and dropped it down into the black place where all the naughty thoughts come from. Then back came the wind and carried the paper angel out through the door and back to the Christmas tree where he had been swinging round and round—do you remember?—when this story began. And it hung him up on one of the branches again by the little bit of red silk.

And what do you think was the very first thought in Sally's head when she woke up the next morning, and saw Michael sitting up in his cot? Why, 'SHARE', of course!

'Michael,' she said, 'you can play with my tea set today.' And she jumped out of bed and kissed him.

Marjorie E. Procter

THE LITTLE FIR TREE

A Christmas story

Once there was a little fir tree which stood in the great forest, in the midst of some big fir trees. The little fir tree was very unhappy because he was not big like the others. When the birds came flying into the woods and lit on the branches of the big trees and built their nests there, he used to call up to them, 'Come down, come down, rest in my branches!' But they always said, 'Oh no, no; you are too little!'

When the splendid wind came blowing and singing

through the forest, it bent and rocked and swung the tops of the big trees, and whispered to them. Then the little fir tree looked up, and called, 'Oh, please, dear wind, come down and play with me.' But he always said, 'Oh no; you are too little, you are too little.'

In the winter the white snow fell softly, softly, and covered the great trees all over with wonderful caps and coats of white. The little fir tree, close down in the cover of the others, would call up, 'Oh, please, dear snow, give me a cap too. I want to play too.' But the snow always said, 'Oh no, no, no; you are too little, you are too little.'

The worst of all was when men came into the wood with sledges and teams of horses. They came to cut the big trees down and carry them away. Whenever one had been cut down, and carried away, the others talked about it, and the little fir tree listened, and heard them say that when you were carried away so, you might become the mast of a mighty ship, and go far away over the ocean, and see many wonderful things; or you might be part of a fine house in a great city, and see much of life. The little fir tree wanted greatly to see life, but he was always too little; the men passed him by.

But by and by, one cold winter's morning, men came with a sledge and horses, and after they had cut here and there they came to the circle of trees around the little fir tree, and looked all about.

'There are none little enough,' they said.

Oh, how the little fir tree pricked up his ears!

'Here is one,' said one of the men. 'It is just little enough.' And he touched the little fir tree.

The little fir tree was happy as a bird, because he knew they were about to cut him down. And when he was being carried away on the sledge he lay wondering, *so* contentedly, whether he should be the mast of a ship or part of a fine city house. But when they came to the town, he was taken out and set upright in a tub and placed on the edge of a path in a row of other fir trees, all small, but none so little as he. And then the little fir tree began to see life.

People kept coming to look at the trees and to take them away, for this was a place where they sold trees. But always when they saw the little fir tree they shook their heads and said, 'It is too little, too little.' Until, finally, two children came along, looking carefully at all the small trees. When they saw the fir tree, they cried out, 'We'll take this one; it is just little enough.'

They took him out of his tub and carried him away between them. And the happy little fir tree spent all his time wondering what it could be that he was just little enough for. He knew it could hardly be a mast or a house, since he was going away with children.

He kept wondering, while they took him in through some big doors, and set him up in another tub on the table in a big bare room. Very soon they went away, and came back again with a big basket which they carried between them. Then some pretty ladies, with white caps on their heads and white aprons over their blue dresses, came bringing little parcels. The children took things out of the basket and began to play with the little fir tree, just as he had often begged the wind and the snow and the birds to do. He felt their touches on his head and his twigs and his branches. When he looked down at himself, as far as he could look, he saw that he was all hung with gold and silver chains! There were strings of white fluffy stuff drooping around him; his twigs held little gold nuts and pink, rosy balls and silver stars; he had pretty little pink and white candles on his arms; but last, and most wonderful of all, the children hung a beautiful white, floating doll-angel over his head. The little fir tree could not breathe for joy and wonder. What was it that he was, now? Why was this glory for him?

After a time everyone went away and left him. It grew dusk, and the little fir tree began to hear strange sounds through the closed doors. Sometimes he heard a child's voice.

He was beginning to be lonely. It grew more and more shadowy.

All at once, the doors opened and the two children came in. Two of the pretty ladies were with them. They came up to the little fir tree and quickly lighted all the little pink and white candles. Then the two pretty ladies took hold of the table with the little fir tree on it and pushed it, very smoothly and quickly, out of the doors across a hall, and in at another door.

The little fir tree had a sudden sight of a long room with many little white beds in it, of children propped up on pillows in the beds and of other children in great wheelchairs, and others hobbling about or sitting in little chairs. He wondered who all these children were; he did not know that he was in a hospital. But before he could wonder any more, his breath was quite taken away by the shout all these children gave.

'Oh! Oh! M-m, m-m!' they cried. 'How pretty! How beautiful! Oh, isn't it lovely!'

He knew they must mean him, for all their shining eyes were looking straight at him. He stood as straight as a mast, and quivered in every needle for joy. Presently one child's voice called out, 'It's the nicest Christmas tree I ever saw!'

And then, at last, the little fir tree knew what he was; he was a Christmas tree! And from his shiny head to his feet he was glad, through and through, because he was just little enough to be the nicest kind of tree in the world.

From Stories to Tell to Children *by Sara Cone Bryant (Harrap, 1922) Slightly adapted.*

TIMOTHY'S CHRISTMAS PARTY

Based on a true story

Timothy was going to have a party after Christmas. He had invited some of his cousins and some of the boys and girls at his school, and specially his friend Michael. There were twelve boys and girls coming to the party.

Timothy's daddy had brought in a fine big Christmas tree and put candles on it. And his mummy had decorated it with beautiful shining balls and golden strings and other lovely ornaments. And she said to Timothy, 'Would you like to give a present off the tree to all the children who are coming to your party?'

'Oh yes,' said Timothy.

'Would you like to come shopping and help me buy them?' asked his mummy.

'Oh yes, please,' said Timothy. So they went out together to the toy shop, and began to buy presents for the children. They bought (*enumerate*). Then Timothy said, 'Oh, look—there is a model space rocket just like the one I had for Christmas. Could we buy it to give to Michael?'

'Yes, of course,' said his mummy; and so they did. Then they brought all the presents home, and Timothy helped his mummy to tie them up in pretty paper with coloured ribbons, and then they hung them on the tree. Then Timothy's mummy went into the kitchen to make good things to eat at the party. (*Enumerate.*)

The day of the party came, and just after breakfast the telephone bell rang. Timothy's mummy went to answer it, and when she came back, she said, 'That was Michael's mummy on the telephone. She says that Michael's cousin Robert has come to stay with him. You remember Robert— he is just about as old as you are. But if Michael comes to tea, he will have to bring Robert too. But that will be all right, won't it?'

'Oh yes,' said Timothy. 'But, Mummy, we haven't got a present for Robert.'

'No more we have,' said his mother. 'And I have so much cooking to do today that I shall have no time to go out and buy one. What shall we do?'

Timothy thought very hard; and at last he said, 'Shall I give Robert one of my presents? I had lots at Christmas.'

'What a good idea!' said his mother. 'You go and choose one while I finish the cooking.'

So Timothy went and got all his presents out and looked at them. He was trying to decide which one to give to Robert. 'There are those building bricks,' he thought. 'I don't like them very much. And there's that rubber ball—I have got one already. Perhaps I could give Robert one of those.' But something inside him seemed to be saying, 'What about your rocket? Wouldn't Robert like that best of all?'

Timothy didn't want to listen to that little voice inside him, because it was the present he liked best himself. But at last he took the rocket and ran down to his mother. 'I want Robert to have this,' he said.

'Very well,' said his mother; and she wrapped it up and hung it on the tree. And soon it was tea-time, and all the children came. They had a lovely tea; and afterwards they went into the room where the Christmas tree was, and it looked so beautiful, with all the candles shining, that they just stood quite still and said, 'Ooh!' Then Timothy began giving out the presents. Michael's eyes sparkled when he saw the rocket. And then Timothy said, 'This is for you, Robert,' and gave him another rocket—Timothy's very own rocket. How pleased Robert was!

At last the time came for all the children to go home, and they all said good-bye to Timothy and his mummy and daddy and 'Thank you for the lovely party.' And the last person to go was Michael's mummy, who had brought Michael and Robert to the party. 'Thank you so much,' she said. 'And thank you specially for giving Michael and Robert both the same lovely present. You know, they get dreadfully jealous of each other; and when I saw Michael's rocket, I thought, "Oh dear, Robert is going to be so jealous, and there will be terrible fights!" But now they've both got the same, and there won't be any fights. I'm so thankful.' And then Timothy was really glad he had given away his precious rocket.

THE FIRST CHRISTMAS TREE

Based on a German legend

It was winter in the Great Forest. All the mice and squirrels were fast asleep in their holes, and the trees kept close to each other for warmth. The wind shook their bare branches, but their roots went deep and safe into the warm earth.

It was very still in the Great Forest. Long ago the charcoal burners had gone into their huts to keep warm. The old women and the children, who had come to gather wood, had gone home with their bundles to the village on the edge of the forest, and were now sitting round their wood fires.

But someone was out in the forest. Down one of the long walks came the Christ Child, looking at all the trees as He passed, to see which was the most beautiful. After Him came a young rabbit, lippity-lippity, and a baby reindeer, trippity-trippity; and a robin with a breast as red as a holly-berry flew from tree to tree as the Christ Child passed, flippity-flippity.

Presently the Christ Child stopped beside a very tall beech tree. It was the biggest and most beautiful tree in all the forest. It had a straight, straight trunk that soared up and up almost out of sight, and every branch was the most perfect shape; snowflakes had settled on the tip of some of them, and the white berries of a mistletoe made a necklace of pearls round its throat.

'Will you come with Me?' asked the Christ Child, touching the silver-grey trunk of the tree gently with His fingers. The tree stooped down to hear Him, He was so little and the tree was so tall.

'Come with you?' asked the tree, looking very thoughtful. 'What will You give me if I do?'

'I have nothing to give,' said the Christ Child. 'But if you come with Me, I will make you a blessing to men.'

'No,' said the tree, shaking her head so that one or two of the berries dropped to the ground. 'I could not come with You. You see, I am the most beautiful tree in all the forest, and it might spoil my beauty if I took my roots out of the ground. Besides,' she whispered, looking at the other trees round, 'what would my friends think?'

So the Christ Child went a little farther, and presently he stopped beside an oak, not quite so tall as the last tree, but very strong and just as beautiful. Her branches stretched like a mother's arms, very wide and protecting, and many little plants and ferns nestled about her roots.

'Will you come with Me?' asked the Christ Child, touching the branches of the oak tree gently with the tips of His fingers. The tree stooped down to hear Him, sweeping her branches towards Him as though she were putting her arms round Him.

'Come with You?' asked the tree, looking rather hurt. 'No, I could not come with You. You see, I am needed here. What would all the little plants do that are nestling around me? And I have a mole asleep in my roots, and a squirrel has his hoard of acorns near my heart. Besides, I have an arrangement with several birds this year who want to build their nests in my branches.'

So the Christ Child went a little farther, and presently He stopped beside a silver birch, just as beautiful as the other trees, but it was only a little tree. It was very slender, and it danced to the music of the wind playing like a harp among the trees.

'Will you come with Me ?' asked the Christ Child, touching the little trunk gently with the tips of His fingers. And the little tree did not need to stoop, she was so small.

'Come with You?' asked the little tree, shivering slightly as if she suddenly felt the cold wind and snow. 'Where do You want to take me?'

'That you will see,' said the Christ Child. 'I only promise that you will be with Me.'

'Oh,' shivered the little tree, looking very scared, 'I could not go somewhere I know nothing about. You see, I am only a little tree, and if I came with You, I might have to grow up, and I don't want to grow up. I like being a little tree; the big trees in the Great Forest look after me. No, I could not come with You.'

So the Christ Child went a little farther, and presently He stopped beside a fir tree, not so little as the last tree, and not so big as the other trees, but just as beautiful.

'Will you come with Me?' asked the Christ Child, touching the trunk of the tree gently with the tips of His fingers. And the tree did not need to stoop to Him; she heard what He said in every one of her branches, right to her tip out in the snow and the wind.

'Yes, I will come with You,' she said, standing very straight. So the Christ Child went down through the Great Forest, and after Him went the fir tree, hoppity-hoppity, and the young rabbit, lippity-lippity, and the baby reindeer, trippity-trippity, and the robin with the breast as red as a holly berry, flying in and out of the tree and all around it, flippity-flippity. And presently they came to the village.

In the middle of the village there was a green, and in the middle of the green the Christ Child and His companions stopped. All the littlest stars came running down from the sky to see what had happened, and they alighted on the tips of the branches of the tree and stayed there. The biggest star of all stood on the tip-top of the tree. And the robin perched under the star and stretched his throat to sing.

When the angels in the sky heard the robin sing, they began singing too. Then all the doors of the houses burst open, and out tumbled the children of the village—big children, little children, middling children; little girls with long fair pigtails and little boys with round rosy cheeks.

When they saw the tree they all said 'Oooh-ooo!' and joined hands and danced round it. Then all the children who had toys shared them with those who hadn't any, because when one person begins to give, everyone begins giving, and the Christ Child and the tree had taught the village how to do it.

Late that night, when all the children had gone to bed and the young rabbit and the baby reindeer had found a warm place to sleep, in somebody's stable, and even the robin was asleep with his head under his wing, a little wind sprang up and shivered through the branches of the fir tree.

'Aren't you cold,' asked the little wind, 'and lonely, all by yourself, far away from your friends in the forest? And aren't you frightened? When all the stars have gone out and Christmas is over, you will be quite alone.'

'And what if I am?' said the tree, and she laughed along her branches. 'And what does it matter anyway? The world is beginning to give, and I want to go on giving for ever with it.'

As she laughed, all the bare branches began to grow, and they covered her warmly with a green blanket, which the fir tree has never lost since that day.

Marjorie E. Procter

THE MAGIC TREE

Once there was a Christmas tree that was not like ordinary Christmas trees. Outside it looked just like other trees, but inside it was quite different. It was a magic tree.

The first person who found out about it was a teacher called Miss Primrose. One night she was standing under the tree looking at its beautiful branches, and she said to herself, 'I wish the tree was covered with lights.' And suddenly, it was!

She thought and thought about it. If the tree could do

that, perhaps it could do other wonderful things too. She thought she would wish for something else, and see what happened. So she went to the tree, which was in the hall of her house, and said, 'I wish there was a big box of chocolates on this bottom branch.' Then she waited; but no chocolates came, and she went away disappointed.

Miss Primrose had a great many things to do to get ready for Christmas. She sent off Christmas cards, and made paper chains for the house, and collected holly and leaves for decorations, and helped with the cooking. She wrote letters, and looked out a good big stocking ready for Christmas morning.

On Christmas Eve Miss Primrose and her family were having a party. All her uncles and aunts were there, and six cousins, and the family from next door. All of a sudden one of the cousins, a little boy called James, said, 'What a lovely tree! I wish there was a big red tractor on it. That's what I want for Christmas.' And sure enough, there was the tractor hanging from a branch, just within his reach. So he took it down and started to play with it. Then everybody got very excited, and started asking the tree for all sorts of things. But they found that it would only give one wish to each person, and that wish had to be for something that was really needed and was a sensible thing to ask for. It really was a most extraordinary tree.

At last all the family had had a present from the tree, and it wouldn't give any more. But it seemed a pity to waste it; so Miss Primrose decided to have another party, and this time to invite all the children she knew, so that they could have a present each from the magic tree. She asked a great many children; some of them were almost strangers, but it seemed a good idea to ask them all, even the little boy who lived opposite Miss Primrose's house, although he wasn't at all the sort of boy she liked. He was usually cross and spiteful, though when he came to the party Miss Primrose noticed that he was shy and didn't speak to anyone.

After tea, Miss Primrose told the children that they could ask for whatever they liked off the tree, but that they would only get what they asked for if it was something sensible and something they really needed. How they enjoyed themselves! Some of the children asked for puzzles and dinky toys, some of them had books, and some of the girls asked for dolls, and got lovely big ones with hair that could be washed and brushed and beautiful clothes. But the little boy from the house opposite wouldn't ask for anything. He was too shy; and when he was asked to take his turn, he wouldn't even speak.

'Go on,' everybody said. 'Why don't you ask for something?' But he just turned away and wouldn't say anything. Then a big girl came and whispered to Miss Primrose, so that no one else could hear.

'Don't worry him,' she said. 'You know he hasn't got a happy home. He hasn't got a father, and his mother has gone away and left him with his grandad. They don't like each other much, so he is very unhappy.'

So Miss Primrose said to the little boy, 'You needn't *say* what you want. Just *think* it, and perhaps the tree will give it to you.'

Then all at once the lights on the tree went out, all except one at the bottom. Under the tree there was a little stable with Baby Jesus in the manger, and Joseph and Mary, and the shepherds coming with their gifts. The one light on the tree shone just over it, so that you couldn't help looking at the scene, and they all gazed at it, wondering what would come next. And as they looked, they heard music. The tune was 'Away in a manger', but the words were different. This is how they went:

> God loves you. He sent you
> This Baby to show
> That He cares about you;
> And wants you to know—

Though others may fail you,
His love is still true.
For ever and ever
God always loves you.

You see, the magic tree knew that what the cross little boy really wanted was someone to love him, and although it couldn't give him that, it could show him where to find it, and the little boy understood that God really did love him, and that Baby Jesus was the best gift of all. Then he felt really happy at last. From that day on, he stopped being shy and cross and spiteful, so that everyone began to love him.

Wasn't that a wonderful present from the magic Christmas tree?

Margaret Sanders

VII

STORIES FROM HISTORY

This is a story about a little boy called Alfred, who lived in our country a very long time ago. He was a prince, because his father and mother were the king and queen. He had three brothers and a sister; but he was the youngest of the family—the baby; and when this story happened he was about five or six years old.

The five children, Alfred and his brothers and sister. loved to play out of doors near their father's palace. But when the weather was wet, or when it was too dark to be outside, they would play in the great hall, and sometimes their mother would read to them out of a big book. This book was full of songs and rhymes and stories and riddles; and it had beautiful coloured pictures all painted by hand, with real gold and silver on them. The children loved their mother to read to them from it.

One day they were looking at the pictures together.

'It is a beautiful book,' said one of the children. 'I wish it belonged to me.'

'So do I,' agreed the other children.

'Well,' said their mother, 'whichever of you learns to read it first shall have it for his very own.'

'Do you really mean it, Mother?' asked Alfred, his eyes shining.

His mother smiled. 'Yes,' she said, 'I really mean it.'

Then Alfred, though he was such a little boy, made up his mind to earn the book. He went to the man who gave him lessons in the palace, and asked him to read the stories and rhymes to him. Alfred's teacher read them over and over again, until at last Alfred had learnt them, and knew them all by heart. Then he took the book to his mother.

'Mother, I can read!' he cried. He opened the book and said the words on every page, so that it looked just as if he were reading them.

Of course, his mother knew what he was doing; but he was the only one of the five children who had tried to earn the book, and so she said that he could have it.

But Alfred was not satisfied with that sort of reading. He set to work to learn how to read properly, and in time he had managed it. And then he had really earned the beautiful book.

When he grew up and became king—yes, he did become king, even though he was the youngest of the family—he did all he could to see that all the people had a chance to learn to read, and also books to read from. And it all began with the beautiful picture-book.

KING ALFRED AND HIS ENEMY

Alfred was the youngest of the children of King Ethelwulf; but his three brothers all died, and so he became King Alfred while he was still quite young. He loved his people very much, and wanted to make them happy. But the first thing he had to do was to conquer some enemies, called Danes, who came from over the sea. They used to come sailing in their long ships with dragon-heads and land in England, and then they would ride about everywhere, robbing and killing and burning. Sometimes the people of the land were able to beat them in battle and drive them away; but they always came back. At other times the Danes were given money, and promised to go away; but still they always came back again.

Alfred was a great general, and he managed to beat the Danes, and their fierce leader, who was called Guthrum. He did it by shutting them up in a city and not letting them have any food. Then he and his men waited till the Danes were so hungry that they gave in.

The Danes all expected to be killed, because that was what people usually did to their enemies in those days when they defeated them.

But they had a great surprise. King Alfred sent a message to Guthrum inviting him to come and stay at the royal palace and bring thirty of his best men with him. When they came, King Alfred treated them, not as conquered enemies, but as friends. He gave them all wonderful meals, which they must have been very glad to have, and splendid presents to take away. He told them that that was the Christian way— the way God wants people to live, as friends and not enemies. The Danes all decided to live the Christian way too; it seemed so much better than the old way of killing each other. So at a special ceremony water was poured on their heads as a sign that they were Christians.

Then Alfred and Guthrum, who were now friends, made a treaty together—a solemn promise. Alfred said that the Danes could live in peace in a part of the land; and Guthrum's promise was that he and his men would live peaceably, and not kill or burn or steal any more. Everyone expected that the Danes would break this promise too, as they had always done in the past. But they never did. They found that Alfred's way, the Christian way, was truly the best. And that is how Alfred conquered the Danes, by friendship and not by war.

THE KING AND THE SPIDER

There was once a brave Scottish king called Robert the Bruce. He was a good general; but he could not win battles. Six times he led his men against the enemy, and six times they were defeated and had to run away.

The sixth time, while King Robert was making his escape, he came to a poor man's hut and went into it to find shelter and to rest. He sat there, feeling very sad, and not knowing what to do next. If he led his men into battle a seventh time, would they have to run away again?

As he sat there, he looked up and saw a spider swinging from a long thread. It was trying to fix this thread to a beam so that it could spin its web; but it could not reach the beam. It tried again and again, while King Robert watched. He counted the tries—one, two, three, four, five, six, *seven!* At the seventh try it managed to reach the beam and stick its thread to it. Now it could start to spin its web, in which it could catch flies for its dinner.

'That spider is just like me,' said King Robert to himself. 'It was beaten six times, like me; but the seventh time it won. Perhaps if I tried just once more, I should win a battle.' He felt that the spider had given him new courage and hope. He called his men together, and they marched out against the enemy. And this time they won. How grateful King Robert was to the little spider which had given him the courage to go on.

THE LITTLE FRENCH GIRL

This is a story about a little French girl. Her father was a farmer, and she lived in the country in France a very long time ago. She did not go to school, because in those days there were no schools for country children; instead, her mother gave her lessons. But she did not teach her to write and read; Joan's lessons were about cooking and spinning, weaving and sewing, and she learnt how to do all these things very well, and was a great help to her busy mother.

She helped her father in the work on the farm too. But her life was not all work. She and the other children had wonderful playtimes. They used to run races, and Joan was one of the quickest runners, and often won. They went for picnics too, and on holidays they loved to go into the woods and dance round a special tree which they called the 'fairy tree'. They all had great fun, and by the end of the day they were tired out, and Joan was glad to go home and slip into her little bed and fall asleep.

Everyone loved Joan, because she was such a kind little girl, and always doing kind and loving things for people. One night, when she and her family were sitting round a table eating their evening meal, there came a knock at the door. Outside was a poor old woman, a beggar, who was tired and cold and hungry and had no home to go to. In those old days there were many people like that.

Joan's father and mother invited the poor old woman in and gave her a good meal and let her sit by the fire and rest and get warm. But presently it came towards bedtime.

'I wish we could ask the old woman to stay here for the night,' Joan's mother said to her father. 'But we have no bed for her.'

Little Joan heard what they were saying, and she went up to her mother and whispered, 'Let her have my bed.'

'But where will you sleep, child?' asked her mother.

'On the kitchen floor by the fire,' said Joan. 'I shall be quite warm there.'

So her parents let her do that kind deed. The old woman slept in Joan's little bed, and Joan slept on the kitchen floor. I expect her mother put down some rugs or old clothes to make a soft bed, don't you?

When Joan grew up, she loved her country as much as she had loved people like the old beggar woman. One day you will hear the story of how she saved France from her enemies. She was known as Joan of Arc (Jeanne d'Arc).

HONEST ABE

In the country called America, not so very long ago, there was a man called Abraham Lincoln. He was called Abe for short; and he had another name too. People called him 'Honest Abe', because he would never do anything that was not straight and honest. Which was why the people of America chose him to be their chief man, or President, because they knew that they could trust him always to tell them what was true and to do what was right.

This is a story about the sort of thing Abe Lincoln did which made people trust him. When he was a young man, he had not very much money, and he took a job in a shop, selling things to people.

One day a lady came into the shop to buy something.

'How much is this?' she asked.

So Abe told her the price, and she paid it and went away. That evening, when the shop was shut, and the money was counted up, there was too much there. Abe thought, and then he realised that he had charged the lady too much.

'I must take it back to her,' he said. But the other people in the shop laughed at him.

'It's a long walk,' they said, 'nearly three miles. And it's a very little money. Why not leave it alone and say nothing?'

But Abe felt that that would not be honest. Tired as he was after his day's work, he walked to the lady's house and gave her back the money. And only after that did he go back to rest and have his supper.

THE MAN WHO LOVED ALL CREATURES

Abraham Lincoln, who was President of the United States of America, was a very kind man who loved all creatures. However much he had to do, he was never too busy to help any who were in trouble, even the very smallest ones. Here are two stories about what he did.

Once Abraham Lincoln and a party of his friends were out riding on horseback. It was a very hot day, and the horses grew thirsty. So when the riders came to a nice shady place, where there were wild plum and crab-apple trees, they decided to stop for a rest and give their horses a drink.

When they had rested long enough, they got ready to start off again; but Lincoln was not to be found anywhere.

'Where is Lincoln?' everyone was asking.

'I saw him a few minutes ago,' said one of the party. 'He had found two little birds who had tumbled out of their nest, and he was looking about to find the nest and put them back safely.'

Presently Lincoln came back, looking very happy because he had found the nest. His friends laughed at him for taking so much trouble over two little birds; but Lincoln said, 'If I had not put those birds back in the nest where the mother can feed them, I could not have slept all night.' He would have been lying awake thinking of the two poor little things lying on the cold ground and crying for their mother.

Another day he was walking along with a friend when they saw a little beetle lying on its back. It was trying and trying to turn over, but once beetles have turned on to their backs, they cannot turn over again. So there it lay, waving its legs in the air. Lincoln stooped down and gently turned it over, so that it could run away. 'You know,' he said to his friend as they walked on, 'if I'd left that beetle struggling on his back, I shouldn't have felt right inside. I wanted to put him on his feet and give him a chance.'

He must have had a very kind and loving heart to care so much for baby birds and beetles. No wonder the people made him their President, the man who has to care for all the people of America.

THE LITTLE GIRL AND HER LESSON

A little girl called Victoria was one day having a lesson with her teacher. The lesson was about kings and queens, and the teacher was telling Victoria about them, and how some of them were good and some of them were bad. Then she went on to talk about the kings and queens of England, and how they all belong to one family. And as the teacher talked, Victoria began to understand something very surprising— the teacher was talking about Victoria's own family. She belonged to the royal family of England.

The teacher went on talking, and presently Victoria was even more surprised. She began to realise that she herself would be the next queen of England.

'Shall I really be queen one day?' she asked. She could hardly believe it.

'Yes,' said the teacher. 'When your Uncle William dies, you will be the next to sit on the throne of England.'

Perhaps you think Victoria was pleased to find out that she was to be a queen. But she was not. She was very frightened—so frightened that she began to cry. How could she ever take on such a difficult task? But she saw that it had to be. She remembered what her teacher had said about good and bad kings and queens, and she made up her mind then and there that she would be a good queen.

She began from then on to get ready to be queen. She worked very hard at her lessons—her reading and writing and sums and drawing and singing and all the things that little girls learnt in those days. And all the time she grew bigger and bigger, till at last she was quite a young lady, though she was not yet grown up.

Then, very early one morning, while Victoria was still asleep, there came a knocking at the door of the house where she lived. Outside were two gentlemen, who said they wanted to come in and see her.

'But it is so early,' said the sleepy person who opened the door.

'We must come in,' said the two gentlemen. 'We have brought an important message for Her Majesty the Queen.'

The Queen! That was different. Everyone began hurrying about, and presently Victoria felt her mother's hand shaking her. 'Get up quickly and go downstairs,' she said. 'There are two gentlemen to see you, and they have news.'

Victoria guessed what the news must be. She did not stop to dress. She pushed her bare feet into bedroom slippers, put on a warm shawl over her nightdress, and then went down just as she was, with her hair hanging over her shoulders. And when she came into the room where the two gentlemen were, they knelt down before her and greeted her as their queen.

So then she was able to begin to carry out the promise she had made to be a good queen. She married a foreign prince from Germany, called Albert, who was a very kind man and helped her very much. They had nine children and they were all very happy together. And today we still talk about good Queen Victoria, who reigned for sixty-four years, longer than any other king or queen of England, and who was so much loved by all her people.

THE SHEPHERD'S DOG

A story about Florence Nightingale

You will often hear people talking about Florence Nightingale. She was a lady who nursed people who were ill, and taught other women how to be nurses too.

Even when she was quite a little girl, she loved looking after sick people. She would pretend that her dolls were ill, and put bandages on them and give them medicine. And if any of the family pets were ill, she looked after them too. But best of all she liked to go to homes where there was illness and help to make the sick people better.

One day she happened to meet a shepherd whom she knew; and she found him very sad. 'My old sheep dog Cap has hurt his leg,' he told her. 'It's pretty bad, and I'm afraid it won't get well. The only thing to do is to put him to sleep. But I shall miss him terribly. He is my best friend—and who will help me with the sheep when he is gone?'

Florence was very sorry to hear this sad story. She went and looked at Cap. His leg was certainly very bad. But perhaps if she took great care of him, she might be able to make him better.

'Please,' she said to her friend the shepherd, 'may I see what I can do?'

The shepherd said she might; so she bandaged Cap's bad leg, and kept coming every day to look at it and put on new bandages and do anything she could to make it heal up. And bit by bit the leg began to get better. At last Cap could stand on it again, and in time he was well enough to go out and help his master round up the sheep once more. How grateful the shepherd was to his little friend Florence. And how glad she was that she had been able to help. It made her want to go on and on nursing sick people.

THE LITTLE PRISONER

Another story about Florence Nightingale

This story is about something which happened to Florence Nightingale when she was grown up. She had decided to be a nurse, and she went out to another country where the British soldiers were fighting against the Russians. The wounded soldiers were taken to a hospital, and when Florence arrived there with some other ladies they were terribly ill and miserable, and many of them were dying. But she and the other nurses cared for them, and they began to get better. The wounded soldiers loved Miss Nightingale. They called her 'the lady with the lamp', because she used to walk past all their beds every night carrying a lamp, and speak to one soldier or nod to another as she went by. Just to see her made the soldiers feel better; she could not speak to them all, but they used to see her shadow as it passed them, and that gave them a feeling of comfort too.

One day, when some wounded men were being brought in, Florence Nightingale saw among them a little boy. She was so surprised to see him that she asked who he was.

'He is a Russian—an enemy,' she was told. 'He was wounded when we took him prisoner, so we brought him here.'

The little Russian boy was cared for till he got better, and Florence Nightingale used to talk to him and find out all about him. She found that he was an orphan; his father and mother were dead, and there was no one to look after him or see that he went to school. So, although she had so very many things to attend to, she decided that she would look after this little lost boy and see that he learnt his lessons. And that is what she did.

At last the war was over, and all the wounded had gone from the hospital; and the time came for the nurses to go back to England. And who do you think went on the ship with Florence Nightingale? Why, the little Russian boy. She felt she could not leave him behind. You can imagine how grateful he was to her. One day one of his teachers said to him, 'Where will you go when you die, if you are a good boy?'

'To Miss Nightingale,' said the boy. She was the person he wanted to be with most of all.

ALPHABETICAL INDEX OF STORIES

SUBJECT INDEX

The stories are listed in order of length in each section

WORKING TOGETHER